'I'm a doctor.'

James opened his eyes wide. 'A doctor?' His mouth gaped in disbelief. 'A doctor?' he repeated. 'A medical doctor?'

Lisa looked down at the big ferryman whose feet were hanging over the end of the couch. Why did this local yokel aggravate her so? He was only a sailor, and yet he acted as if he was the one who owned the island.

'Yes,' she answered shortly. 'A medical doctor.' She was quite surprised that he should know the difference.

'Have you any proof?'

Dear Reader

Margaret O'Neill has written a quartet based around Princes Park Hospital, and CHRISTMAS IS FOREVER launches the four books, which will appear in following months. Poppy works on the paediatric ward, while Jennifer in SECOND THOUGHTS by Caroline Anderson works in Paediatric Outpatients, so plenty of babies and children this festive month! Animals, too, in CELEBRITY VET by Carol Wood, finishing with a Scottish island cottage hospital in CURE FOR HEARTACHE by Patricia Robertson. All home-grown stories to wish you a very merry Christmas.

The Editor

Patricia Robertson has nursed in hospitals, in district health, and abroad. Now retired, she is incorporating this past experience in her Medical Romances. Widowed with two daughters, her hobbies are gardening, reading and taking care of her Yorkshire Terriers. She lives in Scotland.

Recent titles by the same author:

TO DREAM NO MORE
HEART IN JEOPARDY

CURE FOR HEARTACHE

BY

PATRICIA ROBERTSON

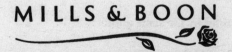

MILLS & BOON

MILLS & BOON LIMITED

ETON HOUSE, 18–24 PARADISE ROAD
RICHMOND, SURREY, TW9 1SR

*First published in Great Britain 1993
by Mills & Boon Limited*

© Patricia Robertson 1993

*Australian copyright 1993
Philippine copyright 1993
This edition 1993*

ISBN 0 263 78380 4

*Set in 10 on 11 pt Linotron Times
03-9312-56492*

*Typeset in Great Britain by Centracet, Cambridge
Made and printed in Great Britain*

CHAPTER ONE

LISA HALLIMAN stood alone at the top of the slipway waiting for the ferry to take her over to the island of Bruig off the west coast of Scotland.

The sea was grey and forbidding and the sky hung above her like a cloak that threatened to fall down and engulf her. Involuntarily Lisa shivered and wondered if the hostile weather was a sign that it had been a mistake to come here.

All her life she had lived in towns or cities. This land with its majestic skyscapes and superb scenery was alien to her.

And yet — its suppressed passion called to something deep inside her. Here was a land as hard as her cold blue eyes — a land that would brook no deceit. Only truth would be enough.

An exhilaration gripped her so that she laughed out loud, a white figure stark against the dark sky, strands of her long blonde hair blowing across her face, quartering it — the smooth high brow, the deep-set blue eyes, the red lips, the firm chin. The wind caught the white scarf at her throat, streaming it behind her. The soft white material of her blouse and straight skirt clung to her as if to protect her. The brown legs were long and the white shoes fitted her feet as only expensive ones could. Her white shoulder-bag swung against the sports car of the same colour, parked beside her.

Lisa could see the island, grey across the grey sea. Her momentary doubts left her. This island was hers, and a sense of power increased her exhilaration.

She could see the ferry coming now. It seemed small

against such an impressive backdrop and she almost resented its intrusion.

James McKinnon, standing at the bow, watched the small figure grow larger as the ferry approached the mainland. He knew who she was — she was expected — Lisa Halliman, the daughter of their absentee landlord, Charles Halliman, who had left the island to her in his will. James had seen photographs of her in the local newspaper.

The lips of his wide mouth compressed. His grey eyes were the colour of the sea. His square jaw tightened, the nostrils of his straight nose flared. He just missed being extremely handsome. Perhaps it was the wideness of his mouth. He was like the backdrop behind him — strong and harsh.

The wind that had caught at her clothes blew his dark hair restlessly about his head. The powerful shoulders stretched the navy blue seaman's jersey as he caught up the rope. The navy corduroys hung low on his lean hips, fitting his thighs as if they were part of him. Centuries of Highland forebears stretching back to the Norwegian invaders had given him his fair, almost white skin.

'Jamie! Are you ready now?'

James looked up at the wheelhouse and his rather harsh features softened slightly as he nodded to his father, Duncan McKinnon, master of the *Ramsay Lass*, who brought the ferryboat smoothly to the slipway. The end of the boat clattered down and Hamish Munro, a big red-headed man, drove his van off with a, 'See ye in the morning, Jamie,' and a wave of his hand.

The van obscured the white sports car which swept on to the ferry without waiting for James to signal it. It came too fast on the damp deck and slewed as Lisa braked, its rear catching James and knocking him over. A big man, he fell heavily. They all heard the crack as his head hit the deck and saw the blood that flowed from a gash on his forehead.

It was the wing-mirror that showed Lisa what had happened. Angus, the other ferryman, stood stunned, his face as white as his hair. It was Duncan who rushed from the wheelhouse to help his son.

Lisa climbed from the car as if in slow motion. Had she killed the ferryman? Shock blanched her features.

It had started to rain. The blood on the injured man's still face mingled with the raindrops, riveleting it into divided streams.

'Jamie, lad.' Duncan knelt beside his son, the lines on his face deepening with anxiety.

Lisa snatched the scarf from her neck and, bending, wrapped it quickly round the bleeding forehead. The blood oozed through the silk.

James opened his eyes and looked straight up at her. She appeared like an angel, beautiful, with her golden hair, fair skin and white clothes. For a moment he was disorientated. He wanted to touch her, see if she was real.

'Help me get him into the car.' Her voice was sharp with arrogance, or so it seemed to James, where, in actual fact, her voice was sharp with shock.

His head was throbbing and his vision inclined to blur, but he managed to raise himself into a sitting position, which did not help his dizziness. I'm damned if I'm going to be sick, he swore to himself, fighting the nausea which threatened.

'Thank God,' Duncan said. 'I thought the lassie had killed you.'

James managed a smile which was more of a grimace.

'It'll take more than an Englishwoman to kill me,' he muttered. Only his father heard him as he and Angus helped James to his feet.

The rain was wetting the red seat of the sports car. Lisa hurried to raise the roof.

'Get him in here,' she ordered.

The three men glanced at her. She was a far different figure from the smart young woman who had waited for the ferry to arrive. Her clothes were wet and her long hair in streaks about her face. Only the cold blue eyes were the same.

She appeared untouched by what she had done. Only the tightness of her jawline betrayed her tension, but the men did not see this. They saw an arrogant, unfeeling woman more interested in keeping her car seats dry.

'Damn fool of a woman,' James said sharply. 'Don't you know any better than to drive on to a ferry without waiting for instructions?'

He pushed himself to his full six feet two inches in height and seemed to tower over her even though she was five feet ten herself.

Lisa hid her surprise at the authoritative way he held himself and the presence he seemed to command, but she was not awed by him.

'Get into the car.' She could be authoritative herself when necessary. 'I'll take you to the hospital where you can get that. . .' she nodded towards his gash '. . .stitched and someone can check you over.'

'There's a hospital on the island,' Duncan said. 'We'll lose the tide if we don't hurry.'

'I can look after myself,' said James curtly.

'Don't be a fool,' she said as he staggered and had to clutch at her outstretched hand to save himself from falling.

She flung the car door open, 'Get in. I'm getting soaked.'

He gave her a look which said, So what? and climbed into the passenger seat. It was cramped, but he did not want to bend to push it back to accommodate his long legs. He felt he would be sick if he did.

'Try waiting until we dock before you leave the ferry when we arrive,' he said in a tight voice.

Lisa had taken her seat beside him. She ignored his words. The smell of oil from his fisherman's jersey mingled with her expensive perfume in the confines of the car. Wisps of steam rose from them both so that by the time they arrived they looked as if they had been in a steam bath.

'Don't you think you should clear the windows?' he said, giving her a disparaging 'Woman drivers' look.

'Leave the driving to me,' she said through gritted teeth as she cleared the windows with the car's blower.

Duncan appeared at her window. She wound it down.

'I'll see you later at the hospital, Jamie,' he said.

'I'll probably be at home,' James replied, giving his father a reassuring smile. With a nod to Lisa, Duncan returned to the wheelhouse.

The car bumped from the ferry on to the slipway. James screwed his eyes up in pain. He must be suffering from concussion, he thought. Damn the woman. He had a good mind to sue her.

'You'll have to direct me,' Lisa said shortly. He was making her feel uncomfortable. It was not what he said, but his presence in the car that was disturbing her. And it was not because he almost seemed to fill it. It was something else. There was an instant attraction which made her breathe more quickly.

Lisa had met quite a few men in her twenty-nine years and she was not a virgin, but she had never been stirred like this. She glanced sideways at him. He looked like a wounded soldier with that white scarf, streaked with blood, his white face and closed eyes.

She had a sudden urge to touch his face and to cover this unusual feeling she said, 'You'd better tell me which way to go,' more abruptly than she normally would have spoken.

'Turn right at the top,' he said coldly.

They were following the coast road. The distant mountains rose to the right, the grass on either side of the road was grey-green beneath the sky, which had lost its blackness and now was as grey as the sea. The windscreen-wipers whish-whished the rain, blurring and sharpening, blurring and sharpening her vision.

James opened his eyes. Lisa had pushed her wet hair behind her ears so that it hung down her back nearly to her waist. She looked like a mermaid and he had a vision of her sitting on a rock, her wavy hair covering her nakedness. The darkened interior of the car softened the angularity of her face, but did nothing for the blue eyes which glanced at him coldly.

'Well?'

This arrogant tone, coupled with the desire his fantasy had roused, aggravated him. He was the injured one and she made him feel it was his fault and that he was just a nuisance.

'Follow the road round. It'll take you to Rothvegan. The hospital's there.' His voice was hostile.

She owed him an apology, but the words would not come. They stuck in her throat, caught there by his unfriendliness.

Lisa concentrated on her driving. The hands on the wheel were fine-boned, but firm. James glanced at her again. She was older than he had at first thought, nearer thirty than twenty. There was pride in the way she carried her head and competence showed in the manner with which she handled the powerful car.

This was no soft, melting blonde. This was a tough, assured woman and he was intrigued.

It was now evening and the afternoon light had darkened further. The headlights were on and they picked out the sign announcing that they were about to enter Rothvegan. Street-lights yellowed the darkness and jaundiced the stone houses — thick-walled and substantial — built to withstand the gales which sometimes swept the island.

They descended into the town.

'Why didn't you come on the mainland ferry?' James asked, curiosity softening his hostility.

'Does it matter?' She was not going to tell him that she had missed the mainland ferry and had been told of the smaller one which ran from Easter to the end of summer.

'Not in the slightest,' he said, hoping she would reach the hospital before he was sick. 'Turn left here,' he told her. 'The hospital is just at the end of this road. You'll be able to see the drive in a minute.'

The street-lighting was not particularly good and she would have missed the entrance if he had not warned her in advance. The hospital signs needed painting. She turned into the drive and expected to see a modern hospital with signs directing the public to the various departments, but all she saw was a single-storeyed building, crescent in shape.

'Is this it?' she said in a disbelieving voice, thinking the bang on his head must have distorted his sense of direction.

'Yes,' he answered shortly, his dislike of her back in full force.

'Does it have a casualty department?' Disbelief was still there in her voice. She had stopped the car, but the engine was still running.

'Drive round to the left. You'll see it then.' Suppressed anger made his head throb. 'And if you don't want your upholstery to smell, you'd better be quick. I'm going to be sick.'

Within a minute she had the car at the casualty

entrance and only had time to see that an ambulance, which looked as if it should be in a museum, was parked in a space reserved for it, before she stopped the car and had James out.

She held his head as he was sick at her feet. Vomit splashed her legs and shoes. She pulled a damp tissue from her pocket and wiped his mouth. It was all accomplished without a word being spoken, which surprised James. He had expected her to complain, and a reluctant, 'Sorry,' left his lips before he could catch it back.

Lisa did not answer, just supported him through the doors, his arm round her shoulders. He was leaning heavily upon her. The acrid smell of vomit was stronger than her perfume and she felt she might be sick herself.

There were a few seats in the small reception area, but no one behind the counter. Lisa lowered James on to one of the chairs, eyeing it doubtfully. It looked as old as the ambulance. She went over to the counter, unwilling to admit that the removal of his arm from about her shoulders had left a coldness she did not want to analyse. There was one of those bells that you banged the top of on the counter. Lisa gave it a few hearty rings. She was becoming worried about James.

A woman of about fifty appeared from a door at the back. 'Can I help you?' she asked, peering over the top of her glasses, her brown eyes interested. She was as tall as Lisa, but her figure had thickened. Her hair was brown, streaked with grey and pulled back into a bun. She wore a pink tweed skirt and a white blouse.

'Is this a hospital?' Lisa's tone was arrogant, and her blue eyes were cold.

'Yes, it is,' Janet Cameron replied calmly, undisturbed by Lisa's attitude.

'I have a patient for you. He fell on the ferry and

cracked his skull. He has a deep cut on the right side of his forehead that'll need stitching.'

'I see.' Janet left the counter and appeared through a door beside it. She glanced towards James. Her face blanched with shock. 'Jamie,' she gasped, hurrying forward.

'Hello, Janet,' he murmured, longing to lie down.

'You can tell me what happened later.' Janet rushed back into the office and returned with a wheelchair. James was in it before Lisa could help. She followed as Janet pulled the chair backwards through the swing doors into what was little more than a large treatment-room. Quickly Janet helped James on to one of the two couches. He closed his eyes as his head touched the pillow.

'I'm afraid you'll have to wait, James,' said Janet, as she took a piece of clean linen and bathed James's face. 'Alistair's delivering Mrs Muir.'

'I can't believe what I'm hearing,' Lisa said in a shocked voice. 'Don't you have another doctor?'

Janet looked at Lisa. Spots of blood and vomit had marked her white clothes and the rain had creased them. Her hair was still wet. Another woman would have looked bedraggled, but not Lisa. There was something distinctive about her. Perhaps it was the proud carriage of her head, or the directness of her cold blue eyes. Janet was impressed, but did not show it.

'This is just a small island hospital,' she said and glanced down at James, who frowned. 'One of our doctors has a couple of days off. If we get anything urgent it's flown to the mainland.' She had reached for a plastic apron and was tying it around her waist. 'The staff and myself can usually deal with minor injuries.' She looked pointedly at Lisa. 'I can look after Jamie now. Thank you for bringing him in.'

Lisa ignored the dismissal. 'Do you have suturing

equipment here?' She glanced round the treatment-room, a doubtful expression on her face, feeling as if she had slipped back in time. There was an electric steriliser, covered dishes and drums, which, Lisa assumed, contained dressings. Bandages were in a pile on the bottom of a trolley.

'Yes.' Janet's reply was short. She was rapidly coming to dislike this young woman. 'Now, if you wouldn't mind going. . .'

'Do you have a blood-pressure machine?'

Janet just nodded.

'Get it. And get a nurse to set up for stitching. I'm a doctor.'

CHAPTER TWO

JAMES opened his eyes wide. 'A doctor?' His mouth gaped in disbelief. 'A doctor?' he repeated. 'A medical doctor?'

Lisa looked down at the big ferryman whose feet were hanging over the end of the couch. Why did this local yokel aggravate her so? He was only a sailor, and yet he acted as if he were the one who owned the island.

'Yes,' she answered shortly. 'A medical doctor.' She was quite surprised that he should know the difference.

'Have you any proof?' He would have sat up, only he knew he would be sick if he did so.

Lisa delved into her shoulder-bag and drew out a letter — it was addressed to Dr Lisa Halliman — and handed it to James.

He glanced at it and handed it not back to Lisa, but to Janet.

'Lisa Halliman.' The older woman looked afresh at Lisa. 'Not Charles Halliman's daughter?' Her eyes were as hostile as James's had been.

'Yes.' Janet's unfriendliness did not bother Lisa either. 'Now that we've cleared that point up, have you a sphygmomanometer?'

For answer, Janet crossed to another trolley and lifted the machine from the bottom. Returning, she handed it to Lisa with the stethoscope.

'You'll need to take your sweater off,' Lisa told James with a nod to Janet. 'The sleeves are too thick.'

As Janet helped James, he said, his words muffled as

the jersey was pulled over his head, 'I don't think much of your bedside manner, Doctor.'

'I didn't hear that,' Lisa said, though she had. 'Perhaps you'd repeat it if it's relevant.' She needed to control the surge of desire that the sight of his perfectly proportioned chest and shoulders was rousing in her. He was the most sexually attractive man she had ever met.

I'm just sex-starved, she chided herself, struggling to subdue her rapidly beating heart and endeavouring to hide the effect he was having upon her.

Fortunately, his head had been inside his jersey when the desire had flared in her eyes. It was an impervious face she presented to him when he repeated his words.

'I should think my competence as a doctor would be of more concern to you than my bedside manner.' She put the ear-pieces of the stethoscope into her ears, signifying the end of their conversation.

Her hair hung down on either side of her face as she leaned forward to record his blood-pressure. It hid the relief in her eyes when she discovered it was normal.

James was astonished at the feelings her lovely blonde, silken, wavy hair roused in him. He wanted to grasp a handful of it — run it through his fingers. Thank goodness she was taking off the cuff or his blood-pressure would have gone up.

'That seems to be all right.' She wrapped the cuff and put it back in the machine's box. A tray had appeared while she had been taking his reading; it was for a medical examination which included an auroscope for looking in the ears, an opthalmoscope for looking in the eyes, a patella hammer for testing the reflexes and a pencil torch for checking the dilatation of the pupil.

Lisa lifted the latter. 'I just want to look into your eyes,' she told him.

James grinned, but the grin changed to a grimace as it pulled on his wound.

'Any time, Doc,' he said, his eyes twinkling, his voice deliberately seductive.

Lisa could not keep her face straight no matter how hard she tried, and, as a result, her smile was lop-sided. It made her look younger, and, with her long hair, somehow vulnerable.

Not such a tough cookie, James mused, surprised at how her smile had affected him. He had been prepared to dislike the daughter of Charles Halliman, but found he was attracted to her instead.

Lisa was testing the reaction of his pupils to light. 'Everything seems in order,' she said. She knew she should check his eyes with the opthalmoscope, but did not want to. The closeness of her face to his that this would necessitate would. . . But she must do it and proceeded to, her heart galloping again to such an extent that she was sure it would leap out of her mouth, and instinctively she compressed her lips.

Once more her hair hung about his face, enclosing them in a light yellow curtain. It created an intimacy which brought a flush to his cheeks, and the scent of her perfume did not help. James had an insane desire to pull her head down and kiss her. The effort required to control his urge increased his flush.

Lisa raised her head. She found her mouth was dry and it was a moment before she could speak. When she felt able, she said, 'I'll just check your ears.' She noted his flush and wondered if he had a temperature, or was it her nearness that had caused it? She was fully aware of the effect she had on men, but in this instance she discounted it. He must have a temperature.

As she picked up the auroscope, the noise of clinking instruments drew her attention. Janet was setting up the trolley, a plastic apron protecting her clothes. Don't tell me she doubles as nurse as well, Lisa mused. What sort of a one-horse hospital is this?

She pushed her hair behind her ears and looked through the auroscope to check for bleeding, inspecting both ears. There was none, so he had not fractured his skull.

Lisa relaxed. The tension she had felt since knocking him down left her, but it left her feeling weak and tired. It had been a strain, maintaining a detached manner.

The trolley rattled up beside Lisa.

'If you require anything else, just ask,' Janet said.

'Would you remove the. . .' Lisa gestured to the stained silk scarf '. . .while I wash my hands?'

Janet nodded. Lisa removed her coat and threw it carelessly on to a wooden chair; it hung half on and half off, its expensive label showing. When she returned the wound was exposed. Janet lifted the towel off the trolley with cheadle forceps and draped it over James's face.

'Getting your own back,' he muttered with a grin before it descended.

Some private joke, Lisa surmised, suddenly feeling the stranger she was. Her eyes were bleak as she looked down upon the wound. It was a nasty gash, but not ragged.

'The scar won't spoil your beauty,' Lisa said, as Janet emptied a fine mersilk with needle attached on to the trolley.

Lisa was quite impressed. It would not have surprised her if Janet had presented her with an ordinary sewing needle and cotton, the place seemed so antiquated.

'Do you have local anaesthetic?' she queried.

For reply, Janet showed her a bottle of Xylocaine in adrenalin two per cent.

'Don't bother with that.' The towel over James's face made little puffs as he spoke each word.

'Tough guy, huh?' she joked. She dried her hands on a sterile towel and arranged further ones around the wound. She glanced at Janet. 'Do you have sterile gloves?' She wondered if the message of AIDS had reached this backwater.

'If you look beneath that towel. . .' Janet nodded to the unused one. . .'You'll find size small.' Her face was impassive.

'Thanks,' said Lisa and slipped the gloves on. 'I'm going to wash the wound now,' she warned James, who grunted in reply. She proceeded to do so with Cetrimide antiseptic. It started to bleed, so she wiped it quickly and looked for the usual disposable bag to put the dirty swab in. Janet pushed a pedal bin forward.

Lisa raised her eyebrow, but trod on the pedal and dropped the swab into it without comment.

'I'm going to stitch the wound now,' she said. Again James grunted. Expertly, she drew the raw edges together. 'I'm putting in quite a few stitches,' she explained, 'So that there won't be any gaps. It wouldn't do to spoil your looks with an ugly scar.'

It was quite a long wound. Lisa could feel James flinch. 'Try to keep your forehead still,' she said as his grimace pulled on the wound. 'You should have had a local anaesthetic, instead of being macho.' Her voice was sharp. She did not like hurting her patients.

'I will next time you knock me over. Ouch!'

Lisa was tying a stitch as he spoke and his accusation caused her to tie it more tightly than she would have done normally.

'Sadist!' James exploded, the word puffing the towel over his face into a small balloon.

'It was your fault,' she snapped. 'I was tying a stitch when you accused me.'

She was mad. The accident, the effect he was having upon her and the hostility she felt in the room all combined to aggravate her. She had had a long drive from London and, having missed the mainland ferry, a further drive to catch the smaller one. She was tired.

James did not speak. The only sound in the room was the click of the scissors as they cut the mersilk. Lisa threw the stitch-holder on to the trolley, upsetting the remains of the antiseptic.

'Done,' she said, lifting the towel from his face. She swabbed the blood from around the wound and examined it.

'A good job?' James looked up at her satisfied face.

'Yes.' Lisa had no false modesty. Then she frowned. His face was drawn and pale. She lifted the can of plastic spray that she had found on the bottom of the trolley.

'Don't put that on,' he said sharply. 'I'll keep it clean.'

Her frown deepened. How did he know what the spray was for? She shrugged. 'Have you had any anti-tetanus injections?' she asked.

'Yes,' he said shortly.

'Well, I think you should have a booster.' Her tone was equally abrupt.

'I only had it three months ago.' He was aggrieved.

'Oh, well, in that case. . .' Her face was stiff. She was not used to having her decisions questioned, especially by a layman.

Lisa turned to Janet. 'This man should be in bed and kept in bed for at least twenty-four hours. I want his blood-pressure, temperature and pulse recorded four-hourly, and any change to be notified to me immediately.' Then she frowned. 'You do have beds in this hospital?'

'Yes.' Janet's face was expressionless. 'You may safely leave. . .' She paused for a moment, then added, 'Jamie in my care.'

Did this woman run the hospital single-handedly? Surely not. Oh, no, of course not, Lisa told herself.

'You'll be at Halliman House, I suppose?' Janet asked.

'Yes.' Lisa would have liked to ask directions, but Janet's face was stiff. 'You know the number?'

'It's in the book,' said Janet.

'Right.' Lisa's expression was cool.

Lisa could feel James looking at her. 'If the accident on the boat was my fault. . .' her tone implied that she did not think so '. . .then I apologise. If there is any recompense I can make?' She splayed her hands.

'The accident *was* your fault.' James's voice was firm, his face unsmiling. Then, after a pause, he said, amusement entering his eyes, 'If I can think of something, I'll let you know.'

She grinned. 'I'm sure you will,' she said wryly.

As she left the hospital, she felt cold, damp and thirsty. Climbing into her car, she decided that a meal before she searched for the house would be a good idea. The smell of James's fisherman's jersey still hung in the enclosed space. She opened the window and turned on the headlights. The car's clock showed seven o'clock. Lisa was surprised. She felt as if it was midnight.

She drove back the way she had come and was soon in the town centre. There was a closed look about it. The shops were shut and few people were about.

There must be a hotel, she thought. The bay was in sight and she drove down towards it. A hotel, the Bruig Arms overlooked the harbour. Lisa parked the car and went to have a look at it. It was closed. A notice pinned to the door said 'Open on April 1st'. Today was March the thirty-first.

Everything must close for the winter, she mused,

becoming hungrier. Then she smelt it — fish and chips, and her salivary glands worked overtime.

She followed the smell up a side-street and there it was — the only lit shop. A group of young people, dressed in jeans and sweatshirts, were lounging outside. The boys whistled as the light from the shop shone on Lisa.

'Need an escort, miss?' one of the bigger boys said with a cheeky grin.

'Or maybe something more?' another said, with sly innuendo.

Lisa had worked on Accident and Emergency for some time so she was used to handling difficult situations.

'No, thanks,' she said with a smile, though her eyes were cool and her tone firm.

They felt it and made no more comments to her, though she heard one of them mutter, 'Toffee-nosed bitch.'

She went into the shop. An Italian woman and her husband were serving. Their olive skins looked out of place and their accents, when they spoke, were alien to the island. Lisa felt a sudden sympathy for them. Were the locals hostile to them? she wondered.

They both smiled and the man gave her an admiring glance as she ordered her fish and chips.

'Brown sauce?' Mrs Farino asked.

'No. Just vinegar, please.'

They wrapped it in newspaper and she bought a pint of milk as well. The young people were still there as she left the shop, but they ignored her.

The heat from the parcel warmed Lisa's hands as she hurried to the car. The smell of the fish and chips swept away any lingering scent of the fisherman's jersey. She ate every minute crumb. 'Damn,' she said out loud. 'I forgot to ask directions to the house.' She wiped her hands on a tissue and started the car. She would look for a phone-box and ring the housekeeper for directions. The lawyer's letter informing Lisa of her inheritance had mentioned a Mrs Fraser.

The rain had stopped, but the street-lighting was dim and the evening dark. Lisa just hoped that the old red boxes would still be in use on Bruig. They were. If it had not been for its red colour, Lisa would have missed it. She parked beside it and searched for coins in her purse, wishing she had stayed on the mainland for the night, but she had written to the housekeeper to tell Mrs Fraser to expect her tonight. If she had stayed on the mainland, she would have missed her encounter with — what was his name? — James McKinnon. She did not want her heart stirred.

Don't be silly, Lisa chided herself as she climbed out of the car. Apart from him being her patient she would be unlikely to see him socially.

She dropped two of her coins as she struggled to open the phone-box door. Why did they have to make them so heavy? she wondered, as she bent to retrieve her money.

Lisa put the coins on top of the box, and, taking the lawyer's letter from her bag, found the telephone number and dialled the house. There was no reply. Perhaps Mrs Fraser had not received her letter. Perhaps she should have used a carrier pigeon, Lisa thought cynically. She was about to replace the receiver when a voice with a Highland lilt said, 'If that's you, Archie McPherson, phoning again to know if Miss Halliman's arrived, the answer is no. And as the last ferry has been and gone I don't expect she will be. So I'll thank you not to be phoning again.'

'Well, if he does, Mrs. . .' Lisa glanced at the letter to find the housekeeper's name '. . .Mrs Fraser, you can tell him that I caught the smaller ferry. This is Lisa Halliman speaking.'

There was a pause, then, 'Oh! Welcome to Bruig, Miss Halliman,' Mrs Fraser said, quite unabashed.

Just those few words brought tears to Lisa's eyes and warmed the bleakness of her heart. She had to swallow before she could speak. Then she said, 'I'm in Rothvegan.Could you direct me to the house?'

'Indeed I can,' said Jean Fraser. 'The house is a mile outside the town. If you're phoning from the place I think, just carry on, on that road until you come to a junction then turn left. There's a turn-off to the house half a mile further on, on the right.'

'Thank you, Mrs Fraser.'

Lisa returned to the car and had no trouble finding her way. She turned into the drive shortly afterwards. She was glad of her powerful headlights, for the drive was in need of repair.

Just when she thought she had missed the potholes, she had to swerve quickly to avoid one and nearly hit one of the trees that lined the drive. These trees she remembered from childhood. She had arrived on an evening similar to this, and in the headlights of their car they had appeared threatening, just as they did tonight.

Lisa shivered. She put her foot down on the accelerator and shot forward, not caring if there were any more potholes, only eager to reach the house.

It came into view suddenly, dark and as menacing as the drive. The moon peered over the clouds and washed it with a pale light. A bright security light suddenly came on as Lisa braked, scattering the stones so that some of them hit the thick walls.

She stepped from the car, locked it automatically and went round to the boot. She had just lifted her suitcase out when the front door opened and Jean Fraser stood silhouetted in its entrance.

She was a woman of medium height and build with a cheerful face. Her hair was grey, worn short and wavy. Her features were not unusual and she would have passed without notice, except for the confidence with which she held her head. Her grey eyes were kind as she ushered Lisa into a square panelled hall. An imposing staircase, its banister carved with an intricate design, swept up one side.

Depression descended upon Lisa. She knew she should not have come. An intolerable loneliness made her eyes bleak, as bleak as the memories this house held for her.

CHAPTER THREE

'I HOPE you'll be happy here, Miss Halliman.' Jean's voice sounded uncertain. Lisa's expression was distant and withdrawn. She looked very like her father, Charles Halliman, the entrepreneur who had died a billionaire.

Lisa was remembering the quarrels between her parents. It had been here, at Halliman House, that a divorce had been decided upon. Lisa had been eight at the time.

Her mother had been a top model when Charles had married her. Lisa could hear again her mother shrieking in this very hall, her voice echoing up to the high ceiling, 'I only married you for your money,' and her father's cold anger as he had replied,

'And I only married you for an heir, and look what you gave me. . .' he had flung out his arm in Lisa's direction '. . .a girl.' The contempt in his voice had been thick and heavy and it had devastated the small Lisa.

It was then that the heartache had started. It lasted throughout her lonely childhood and boarding-school years. It was still there when she entered medical school. Sometimes it was worse, sometimes better, and, occasionally it left her altogether, but it always returned. It was here now.

Her father had married again and had had four children, all boys; the eldest would be about nineteen now. They and their mother had inherited the bulk of his fortune, income derived from the many enterprises started by her father. He had had the vision to see what the public wanted — video shops, music stores, fast foods, package holidays — and had entered into many more ventures that had all been successful.

Lisa had seen him on only two occasions since the divorce. Once, soon after the divorce, when she was nine. 'Don't expect anything from me except a good education,' he had said. 'Your mother has been granted a more than generous settlement to live on, enough to support you both in a comfortable lifestyle. I'll pay for your education.'

The second time, Lisa was twelve. He had visited her at the expensive boarding-school her mother had chosen.

'You'd better make the most of this place,' he had said, 'for I'm not leaving you anything in my will. If you choose a career that entails going to university, I'll support you and give you an allowance to see you through, but that's all.'

Lisa had not replied.

The lawyer's letter had been a complete surprise. She still found it hard to believe that her father had left her this island and a great deal of money besides. It was too unreal.

'Your father had followed your career and was proud of you,' the lawyer told her. 'I think he regretted treating you so badly and hoped this inheritance would make up for it. Your mother also benefits by his will to a considerable amount. I don't know if you know. . .' Lisa hadn't. She hardly ever saw her '. . .but we invested the money your father settled upon her following the divorce and it has enabled her to live in considerable comfort, but now she will be. . .' He had spread his hands. But the inheritance could not heal the bitterness or the heartache.

Lisa had seldom seen her mother who travelled with the jet-set. A generous allowance was paid into Lisa's account, supervised by the lawyers. Her grandparents were dead and her mother's relatives did not want her, so Lisa's school holidays had been spent either at school or with Karen's family. Lisa's blue eyes became bleaker as she thought of her schoolfriend. But she had learnt to suppress thoughts of Karen's betrayal and did not allow them to surface now.

'Miss Halliman?'

Lisa was glad to have her memories interrupted.

'Have you eaten?' Jean asked.

Lisa looked into the troubled grey eyes and smiled. She did not want to alienate the only person who had greeted her with kindness.

'Yes, thank you, Mrs Fraser, but I'd love a cup of tea.'

'There's a fire in the lounge.' Jean gestured in its direction. 'I'll bring you a tray.' She smiled. 'You look frozen.'

Lisa was, but it was not her physical state that made her cold through to her very bones. It was the intolerable loneliness that had crept up on her.

Lisa swept her hair behind her ears, straightened her shoulders, and said to herself, as she had so many times before, Self-pity is a negative emotion. And with the strength of character she had inherited from her father she threw her head up and lifted the bleakness from her eyes. She was once again the assured young woman who had stitched James's wound so expertly.

She went into the lounge and switched on the light. It was a large, high-ceilinged room with four tall windows which were hidden behind long velvet curtains. A large log fire warmed the darkness of the furnishings, which would look severe in the daylight.

Three red velvet two-seater couches were grouped around an oak coffee-table in front of the fireplace. A large picture depicting the Highlands with long-horned thick-coated cows hung above it. Three oak cabinets stood between the windows. Lisa went over to them. Ornaments crammed their shelves. Occasional chairs were scattered about the room. Lisa touched the wallpaper. It was of a neutral shade and felt like silk. Further pictures of Scottish landscapes hung on the walls. The carpet was Persian. The effect was a mixture of the garish and the good. Everything was in perfect condition.

The door opened and Jean came in with a tray, the silver teapot, milk jug and sugar bowl reflecting the china tea-set and plate of home-made scones.

'Your father instructed that the house should be kept in perfect condition,' Jean said, as she put the tray on the coffee-table. 'Even though he never came here.' She could not hide her puzzlement. It showed on her face. 'He even had central heating put in to ensure the damp was kept out.'

Lisa thought it strange as well, but did not comment. 'Would you show me over the house?' she said. 'After I've had my tea?'

'Yes, Miss Halliman,' said Jean. 'Just give me a shout when you're ready.'

After she had gone, Lisa looked at the scones. She was not very hungry, but felt she must eat them. They were delicious. She felt better after the hot tea, and sleepy from the fire. Sighing, she lifted the tray and went into the hall.

'Mrs Fraser,' she called.

Jean came out of a door at the back of the hall.

'Oh, you should have left the tray, miss.' She took it from Lisa. 'We might as well start in the kitchen,' she said and Lisa followed her.

The kitchen was of Victorian proportions. Jean set down the tray and led Lisa back the way they had come.

There was a billiard-room, a dining-room with a large

table that could seat twelve. A huge sideboard stood against one wall. The study was smaller. Lisa opened the desk drawers; they were empty. Books lined one wall. She picked one out; it was a first edition.

Upstairs, there were twelve rooms. It was too dark to see the view from the windows. The master bedroom had a four-poster bed and an *en-suite* bathroom.

'Your father had that put in,' Jean told her.

A fire was burning in the grate. The blue velvet drapes were drawn and Lisa's suitcase lay on a stand provided for it. The Wilton carpet was patterned in shades of blue. A heavy silk bedspread was of the same colour. The furniture was oak and ponderous. It was a man's room.

Lisa crossed to the wardrobe and opened it. It was empty. The whole house seemed as if it was waiting for something, or someone. Lisa had the strangest feeling that her father had preserved this house for her. She could see a man like Jamie in a room like this. Now why should she think of him like that? Ferryboat men did not live in mansions.

Suddenly she was very tired and sat down in the black leather chair beside the fire, feeling the warmth of the leather behind her calves.

'The bed has been kept aired on your father's instructions,' Jean told her. 'And I've put two hot-water bottles in, so you shouldn't feel the cold.'

'Do you look after this house all by yourself?' Lisa asked.

Jean blushed. 'Archie McPherson helps with the heavy work since my husband died eight years ago, and a girl comes from the town twice a week. Archie keeps the grounds in order as well.'

Lisa glanced round the spotless room. 'Well, you've done a good job.'

Jean blushed again. 'Thank you, Miss Halliman.'

'Call me Lisa.'

Jean looked shocked. 'Oh, I couldn't do that, miss. It wouldn't be right.'

'What about a compromise? Miss Lisa, then.'

Jean smiled. 'Very well.' She paused at the door and glanced back. 'What time would you like breakfast?' she said.

'Oh!' Lisa was used to rising early, but she had given up her job as a surgical registrar at the London hospital where she had trained, leaving yesterday, and this would be her first chance for a lie-in for ages, so she said, 'Ten o'clock, I think.' Then she remembered her patient. 'Oh, no. I have a patient at the hospital that I'd better check on.' Then, seeing Jean's surprise, Lisa smiled and said, 'I'm a doctor. One of the ferrymen had an accident, a Mr McKinnon,' she explained.

'Duncan McKinnon?' Jean's face showed concern.

'No, his son.'

Jean's mouth gaped. 'Jamie?' she whispered, her eyes widening.

'Yes.' Lisa frowned, surprised at Jean's reaction. 'You know him?'

Jean swallowed. 'Aye. Everybody knows. . .' There was a slight pause before she added, 'Jamie.' And she left the room quickly, shutting the door sharply behind her.

It appeared that James McKinnon had this effect upon all women, no matter what their age, Lisa thought, remembering Janet Cameron's reaction when James was brought in.

Lisa opened her suitcase and drew out her nightdress. It was white and flimsy, sleeveless, with plenty of lace. She shivered just looking at it. I shall have to get a brushed cotton nightgown, up to the chin with nipped-in cuffs, if I stay, she said to herself, and then laughed.

Her face straightened. Surely she was not thinking of doing so?

Lisa pulled out a brush and crossed over to the dressing-table with its three mirrors. She could see herself trebled and suddenly longed for a sister.

She swept the brush viciously through her hair. Plugs that the rain had caused caught and tugged, bringing tears to her eyes. They washed away the self-pity that threatened.

She plaited her hair into two braids and tied it on top of her head, stripped off her clothes and, wrapping herself in a fluffy white, towelling dressing-gown, she went into the bathroom.

Steam from the hot water caused rivulets to run down the tiles. She soaked until the water became cold. Stepping from the bath, the mat slid so that she stumbled and banged her head on the towel-rail.

James McKinnon's face flashed into her mind. She would phone the hospital tonight to see if he was all right. She should not have required a bang on the head to remind her. Towelled and in her dressing-gown, she rubbed her head ruefully. She had noticed a phone extension beside the bed. She hoped it worked.

It was nine-thirty. Lifting the receiver, she was astonished to hear the operator say, 'Number please.' The island must have its own exchange.

Lisa realised that she did not know the hospital's number and said, 'Put me through to the hospital please.'

The reply of, 'Yes, Miss Halliman,' was a further surprise. Did everyone know she was on the island? Lisa wondered as she waited.

'Matron Cameron speaking.'

Lisa was taken aback for a moment. Janet Cameron, the matron? And she, Lisa, had treated her with scant respect.

'This is Dr Halliman,' she said, deciding that an apology would make matters worse. 'How is James McKinnon?'

'Resting.' Janet's voice was as cool as Lisa's. 'His recordings are normal. You don't need to worry about him.'

'I wasn't worried about him, Matron.' Lisa's tone was brusque. 'I was just doing my duty.'

There was no reply, but Lisa knew that Janet was still there. A nurse of her generation would never put the receiver down on a doctor, no matter how rude that doctor had been.

'Phone me if there's any change in his condition.'

'Yes, Doctor.' Janet's tone was stiff.

'I'll be in tomorrow morning.'

Lisa sighed as she replaced the receiver. She really must stop being so abrasive.

Throwing her dressing-gown on to the chair, she climbed into bed. It had a feather mattress and cocooned her body. Jean had taken off the silk bedspread. A duvet with a navy blue cover and pillowcases to match seemed out of place in this ponderous bedroom.

Lisa turned off the bedside light. A green dragon on a white background glared at her from its base. She turned her face away, too tired for the thoughts which crowded into her mind to take hold.

The room was dark when she woke. Was it the middle of the night? she wondered. It was a moment or two before she realised where she was.

She switched on the bedside light. A brass clock of modern design showed her it was nine o'clock. Throwing back the duvet, she slipped on her dressing-gown and slippers, shivering at their coldness, though the room was warm.

She crossed to the window and pulled back the heavy

drapes. Archie McPherson glanced up from the garden. She looked like an Austrian princess, with her blonde plaits hanging nearly to her waist and her white dressing-gown.

He waved, but she did not see him. She only had eyes for the view. Her bedroom was at the back and overlooked the sea. Mountains rose as if from the waves, stark in the harsh morning light. The clear, almost light sky and the mountains tipped with pink held her with their beauty. She had never seen such a clear light before.

Reluctantly, Lisa turned away. Washed and dressed in a pale blue skirt of fine tweed which she had thrown into her suitcase at the last moment, and a cashmere jumper of the same colour, she brushed her hair and coiled it into a chignon. Her brown slip-ons made no noise on the thickly carpeted stairs.

Jean was in the hall and glanced up as Lisa appeared. 'The fire's lit in the lounge.' She smiled. 'I'll let you know when breakfast's ready.'

Lisa was at the window when Jean returned. The lounge overlooked the gardens which ran from beneath a balustrade towards the trees. There were no flower-beds, just immaculately kept lawns.

Lisa had forgotten to tell Jean that coffee was her usual breakfast, so she was appalled to see covered dishes on the sideboard and toast on the table.

'Just help yourself, Miss Lisa.' Jean smiled. 'You look more rested today.'

Lisa returned the smile and said, 'I am, thank you.' She would have to eat the breakfast.

Jean smiled again. 'I put out coffee and tea for you.' Jean nodded towards the silver pots. 'Not knowing your preference.'

'Thanks. Coffee will be fine.'

'I'll remember,' Jean said as she left.

Lisa lifted the silver lids. Bacon and egg, sausage and mushrooms snuggled together. She took some of each, poured herself some coffee and sat down.

Suddenly she was hungry and ate everything, following it with toast and two cups of coffee. Jean came in as Lisa was finishing her second cup.

'That was the best breakfast I've ever had,' Lisa said.

Jean smiled. 'Thank you, Miss Lisa,' she said as she put the dirty plates on to her tray. 'Will you be in for lunch?'

Lisa had made no plans other than to visit her patient, so she said, 'Yes. About one o'clock be all right?'

'Yes, Miss Lisa.'

She had left her pale blue leather jacket and matching shoulder-bag in the hall. She slipped on the jacket, lifted her bag and stepped from the house into the clear, rain-freshed air.

Her spirits lifted. She looked back at the house and still could not believe it was hers.

The white sports car was splashed with mud. Lisa was behind the wheel in a moment and drove down the drive, carefully remembering where the potholes were.

It did not take her long to reach the town. It looked quite different in the morning light. The shops were open. Mothers with prams were side-stepped by people hurrying along the pavements. Heads turned as the white sports car passed.

The hospital was easy to find. She had just not seen the signposts last night. Lisa drove up to the casualty entrance. The parking spaces were already taken. A battered Range Rover she vaguely remembered seeing last night was parked in a space reserved for doctors.

A smart young woman dressed in a black skirt and white blouse was standing at the reception counter as

Lisa approached. About half a dozen people were sitting in the chairs she had noticed last night.

'Can I help?' Moira Black's voice was as pleasant as her face.

'I'm Dr Halliman. I'd like —— '

'Matron will see you, Doctor,' Moira interrupted as she looked at Lisa with interest. She leaned forward and pointed down the corridor. 'The first door on the right,' she said. 'It has "Matron" printed on the door.'

Lisa thanked her, went in the direction Moira had indicated and knocked on the door.

'Come in.'

Lisa entered.

'Ah, Dr Halliman,' Janet was wearing a navy blue dress with a silver buckle. A small white organza cap was pinned on her head. She looked as if she had stepped from the past.

'How's our patient this morning, Matron?' Lisa said briskly. 'Perhaps you could direct me to the ward?'

'He's not in the ward,' Janet said evenly.

'What?' Lisa's face tightened and her voice was sharp with anger as she said, 'Where is he?'

'I'll take you to him,' Janet said, quite unmoved by Lisa's anger.

She held the door open for Lisa with an impassive face.

Take me to him? Lisa's puzzlement was greater than her anger. Was Janet Cameron going to drive her to her patient? If so, surely it was strange behaviour for a matron, even in an archaic establishment like this.

She followed a step behind. The corridor led away from the reception area and branched left and right at the end. The morning light patterned the stone floor into squares as it shone through the small-paned windows. Lisa could see ward doors.

'How many wards do you have?' she asked, really interested.

'Just two.' Janet sighed. 'Any big cases go to the mainland.' Her tone did not encourage further questions.

Lisa had been so occupied with her thoughts of the hospital that it wasn't until they started to climb the stairs leading from the middle of the corridor that she wondered where they were going, and would have liked to ask, but Janet's stiff back did not invite questions.

This would not have deterred Lisa, but they had turned right at the top of the stairs and paused outside a door. It was the name printed on the door that deprived her of speech. 'DR JAMES MCKINNON'.

Janet knocked.

CHAPTER FOUR

LISA was used to controlling her expression, but this time she could not hide her astonishment. So that was why he appeared different.

The door opened and James stood tall and straight, dressed in well-fitting grey trousers and a white shirt, open at the neck, his black hair curling on its collar. It only needed ruffles at the neck and cuffs to give him the appearance of having stepped from another age. His broad shoulders emphasised the slimness of his hips.

The light was behind him, but Lisa could see how pale he was. The black stitches gave him a rakish look, but it was the effect he was having upon her that stunned her and prevented her from speaking. The attraction she had felt yesterday was back, stronger than before. Her whole body glowed; she was sure it must be bright red and she fought to prevent herself blushing. Oh, isn't he. . .? Before she could find an adequate word — gorgeous, hunky were not enough — the paragon spoke.

'Ah, Doctor.' James's voice was dry as he opened the door wider and gestured for her to enter. 'Come to see your patient?'

James thought her speechlessness was due to the shock she had received at finding he was not a ferryman but a doctor. Maybe that would knock some of the arrogance out of her.

'I'll leave you,' Janet said. Even though the hospital was small, she was short-staffed and had plenty to do. James nodded and smiled.

Lisa had read about women's legs becoming weak when they met an attractive man. Now she knew what they meant. James's smile, even though it was not directed at her, was her undoing. She sat down on the nearest thing available.

As the door closed, James turned and looked at her, his eyes narrowing. She was facing the light and the blondeness of her hair, combined with the blueness of her eyes and clothes, made her look like a summer's day, all fresh and airy. The room around her looked tatty by comparison. Of course, the furniture was old and scuffed. The beige walls needed repainting and the carpet was worn almost to the boards, its brown colour faded where the sun had caught it.

She was undoubtedly an attractive woman. Her figure — how he would like to. . . He quickly swept such erotic thoughts from his mind and kept his face composed, though his eyes were amused at his thoughts.

It was easier to do when he reminded himself that this woman — an Englishwoman at that — owned the island. She could do anything she wanted.

Lisa saw the amusement in his eyes. Was her face red? She tucked a wisp of hair into her chignon and was pleased to feel how cool her skin was. There must be another reason for the laughter in his eyes.

'Do you usually sit on the coffee-table?' James asked.

So that was what was amusing him, Lisa thought mistakenly. 'You're rather short of furniture,' she said smoothly, implying that that was why she was sitting where she was.

She glanced about the room. Besides the coffee-table, there were two armchairs with faded green covers arranged on either side of a brown mantelpiece. A desk under the window was piled with what she supposed were case-notes. A bookcase next to the window was full of well-used medical books.

'Can I get you a cup of coffee?' James was quite unabashed by her scrutiny of his tatty lounge.

'Thank you.' Lisa accepted his offer eagerly. If he left the room she would be able to still her hammering heart.

He opened a door to the left of the fireplace. It must be the kitchen, Lisa thought.

'Why don't you come and help me?' James called. 'Or don't you rich English girls know how to make coffee?'

The mockery in his voice made her narrow her eyes and clench her teeth, but she said sweetly. 'Perhaps you would show me,' and joined him in the small kitchen.

There was an old double white sink and ancient gas stove, no units, just shelves, on which were grouped an assortment of tins—soup, baked beans and tinned meat.

'I take it you're not much of a cook.' She gestured towards the shelves.

He gave a rueful grin. 'You've found me out,' he said.

'It seems I'm finding out quite a bit about you,' she said smartly.

James grinned. She was quick, this lady—very quick.

'First fill the kettle with cold water,' he told her, and did so, putting it on the gas ring, which he lit with a match. 'Then let it boil. While it's boiling, put a spoonful of coffee into each mug.' He reached up to a shelf and picked two mugs—one said, 'I'm the boss', and the other 'You don't have to be mad to work here, but it helps'—and put in the coffee from a jar beside the sink.

The whistling kettle's shriek made Lisa jump. The confined space in the kitchen was not helping her tension. James was close enough to touch.

'I like it black,' she said.

He made the coffee and handed her the mug which declared her the boss. 'Appropriate, don't you think?'

Was that resentment she saw in his eyes? Lisa made no comment, just pointed to his mug. 'I'd say your logo is the more appropriate one.'

Lisa had expected him to smile, maybe ruefully, but nevertheless smile, but his face became harsh.

'That's not amusing.' The hostility Lisa had seen in his eyes when they had first met was back.

He gestured for her to precede him into the lounge.

'I saw the way you looked at our treatment-room and I also saw your barely disguised distaste for. . .' he flung his arm out '. . .these surroundings. Wait until you see the rest of the hospital.' There was a bitterness in his voice which did not lift as he said, 'The Highland Health Board is closing it, by the way. They say it costs too much to run. The sick and injured will have to go to the mainland by sea or air ambulance.'

Lisa did not know what to say. She only felt the passion of his anger and it stirred her.

James drank his coffee and set his mug down with a bang. Rising, he prowled around the room, his body tense, his face tight.

'The authorities don't take the weather into consideration. When storms blow the ships are confined to harbour and the air ambulance can't be used, nor the helicopters.' He stopped his pacing and swung round to glare at her. 'This hospital is small and we treat uncomplicated cases here. Emergencies are dealt with and transferred to the mainland. But without this hospital lives would be lost.'

'It's not my fault,' she blurted out, feeling his anger was directed at her.

'It's Halliman's, though. He could have done something to help the hospital, but he didn't. He didn't care.' He was becoming more intense. 'He could have donated some of his millions to upgrade the building at least, but he was only interested in the island as a possession. He never came here to my knowledge.'

Lisa's eyes became sad as she remembered that day when she was eight, but she did not mention her father's visit.

James was so angry he did not see the expression in her eyes; he only saw the likeness to her father and remembered the only encounter he had had with the billionaire.

In desperation, he had made an appointment to see Charles Halliman after a succession of letters in which James had lowered his pride to beg for assistance in renovating the hospital. He had received no reply.

Charles Halliman had been a big man, as tall as James. His blue eyes, the colour of Lisa's, had been cold and hard and they had looked at James as Lisa seemed to be looking at him now. How had he ever thought he was attracted to this girl?

'I went to see your father six months ago to ask for. . .' the word stuck in his throat. '. . .money.' It came out like a slap. His anger increased, his fists clenched and Lisa leaned back in her chair as if he had struck her. 'He refused me. Said it was the Highland Health Board's job.' He paced the floor. 'Can you imagine it? He, with all that money, refused to donate any of it to the hospital.' His face was sharp with disgust.

Lisa's expression appeared cold and hard to James, but, in reality, it was a defensive mask. It hid the heartache. Anyone who spoke as James had now, spoke the way her father had that dreadful day when she was a child, brought back the anguish.

'Perhaps he was right,' Lisa said. She sounded imper-sonal — unfeeling. There was an arrogant look about her face and he hated her.

'There speaks the father's daughter,' he said with a harsh laugh, his tone derisive.

Lisa shot to her feet, her half-filled mug in her hand. Coffee splashed on to her skirt, speckling it with brown spots. Her face was white with anger and the knowledge that she, with her money, held the fate of his hospital in her hands brought a gleam of satisfaction to her eyes.

She wanted to hit back — do something — anything to soothe the ache in her heart, so she said, 'Don't expect anything from me,' unconsciously using her father's words to her, a dangerous, fierce light in her eyes. 'I'm a chip off the old block as you so rightly said.'

Lisa stalked past him, her back straight, her shoulders squared and left the room, slamming the door behind her. Tears, mostly of rage, stung her eyes as she stormed down the corridor. She hated him, she hated him. The words tap-tapped in time with her footsteps on the stone floor.

She had just reached the reception area when the doors burst open and a woman carrying a screaming child of about a year old rushed up to the counter.

'Help me, help me,' she cried. 'Kevin's finger. . .' She gasped and swallowed, her face white with shock. 'He caught it in the pushchair and it's. . .' She sagged against the counter.

Lisa hurried forward. The young woman, who could not have been more than twenty, looked as if she was going to faint. There was blood on her fair, shoulder-length hair, and on her white anorak. She must have been only about five feet two inches in height, and this made the baby in her arms look bigger than he was.

The half-dozen people in the reception area looked on with interest as Lisa spoke to the mother. They all knew who she was.

'I'm a doctor,' Lisa said, information that raised the onlookers' eyebrows. 'Come with me.' She put her arm

round the young woman's shoulders. Her melodious
voice had a calming effect. Even the child stopped
crying for a moment.

'Send for Dr McKinnon,' she instructed the receptionist. 'And inform Matron.'

In the treatment-room, Lisa seated the young mother
in a chair with the baby, who was now whimpering with
shock, on her knee.

She left the examination for James. There was no
need for her to distress the child; she could see the tiny
finger was almost severed. The blood had congealed,
but, judging from the amount on the child's jacket, he
had lost a fair bit.

She heard the door open and caught the flash of a
white coat. One of the other doctors, she supposed, but
a quick glance told her it was James.

He was no longer the open-necked romantic figure of
her imagination. His black hair was smooth, the incli-
nation to wave tamed. A university tie showed between
the lapels of his white coat. Only the black stitches of
his wound spoilt the picture of the hospital doctor who
would not have been out of place in the Edinburgh
hospital where he had trained — Lisa had recognised his
tie.

'Hello, Kirsty,' he said with that smile that made Lisa
weak in spite of her hatred for him. 'Kevin been up to
tricks?'

'Oh, Dr Jamie.' Relief swept the pinched anxiety
from Kirsty McLean's face. 'I'm so glad it's you.'

Kevin started to cry. Ha! thought Lisa. At least the
baby stopped crying for me. She knew it was unreason-
able and that the child was crying with fright, but
nevertheless. . .

James crouched down beside the mother. 'I'm going
to have to stitch. . .' he gestured to the finger '. . .it
back on.'

Anxiety flared in the mother's eyes and the child, sensing it, screamed and struggled in her arms, the injured hand flailing.

Lisa caught hold of it. 'Hi, Kevin,' she said, smiling gently.

Her voice was soothing, her hand firm. He stopped crying. The tears were wet on his white cheeks, his nose was pinched, and his blue eyes troubled.

James glanced up at Lisa. So she was a good doctor — intuitive — experienced. That did not stop him from hating her.

Lisa saw the coldness of his eyes as he looked at her, but did not care. So he was a good doctor and inspired confidence. That did not stop her from hating him.

Janet joined them.

'We'll need the theatre,' James said, standing up.

She glanced at the injured hand and nodded.

He looked at Lisa. 'Are you trained in anaesthetics?' he asked.

Lisa realised that he was treating her as a colleague. 'You're not. . .' She was going to add. . .repairing this finger here? She knew what skill it required, but she did not complete the sentence. His outraged expression cut her short.

He was right, of course. She should not have spoken so in front of the patient's mother. It galled her to admit it.

Kirsty glanced from one doctor to the other. 'You want to send him away?' Tears fell down her cheeks.

James patted her shoulder. 'No, Kirsty.' His voice was reassuring. 'We'll do it here. When did he last eat?'

Lisa glanced at her watch. It was half-past twelve.

'Eight o'clock. We were on our way to Mum's when this happened.' Tears made Kirsty's eyes seem huge.

'Mum wrapped his hand in a towel, but it came off.' Her voice was rising.

'You did very well.' James gave her a kind smile. 'We'll operate as soon as possible. We'll put him in the side-ward. You'll be able to stay with him. Everything will be all right.' His tone was confident. 'Matron will show you the way and give you a consent form to sign.' When Kirsty looked puzzled, he said, 'We can't operate unless you give your permission.' He smiled reassuringly. 'Matron will explain.'

Janet took Kirsty and Kevin away.

James turned to Lisa. 'How dare you question my decision?' The black stitches looked even blacker as his face became white with anger. 'You know nothing about my professional abilities.' He took a step closer to her. 'You're arrogant and presumptuous.'

Lisa's eyes did not fall. She knew she should apologise, but she was still smarting from their previous encounter. 'I am trained in anaesthetics,' she said, ignoring his anger. 'Perhaps we should put our personal differences aside and think of Kevin.'

Her coolness shook him. Any other doctor would have been subdued and apologetic but not Dr Lisa Halliman. He had to suppress a spark of admiration which threatened to soften his anger.

'Yes,' he said, knowing she was right. He did not know why he did it — it must have been an involuntary action but he put out his hand.

Without hesitation, Lisa gave him hers. It lay slim within his, but the delicate fingers that clasped his were firm. She looked at him with a directness that he had never found in another woman. Her blue eyes were keen with intelligence.

A sudden sense of loss took hold of him. What a pity. Here was a woman he could have responded to. She was exciting, sexy, alluring and clever, but she was

Charles Halliman's daughter. There was a ruthless streak in her.

Lisa saw the sadness that passed fleetingly through his eyes, and felt her heart ache. Here was a man — a real man — upright, forthright, sexually attractive, but he was unbending, unforgiving, un——

A knock was followed by a head round the door.

'Moira said there's an emergency. Want any help?'

A red-headed man as tall as James came in. His eyes lit with admiration when he saw Lisa. 'You don't look in need of emergency treatment,' he said with a grin. Then he saw James's stitches. 'Whatever happened to you, James?' He had laughing eyes and a mouth used to smiling. There was nothing threatening about him. This man would not pull you into his arms, kiss you until your legs melted, Lisa thought. Again, sadness touched her.

'I had an accident,' James said with a rueful grin. 'But I'm not the emergency either. It's Kirsty McLean's Kevin. He caught his finger in his pushchair and almost severed it.' He glanced at Lisa. 'Let me introduce you to the other doctor on the island, Alistair McKay, GP, assistant surgeon, anaesthetist and general dogsbody.' James's tone was affectionate.

Alistair held out his hand. 'Hi,' he said, and then he frowned. 'You're not Charles Halliman's daughter, are you?'

Lisa was not going to apologise for it, or be defensive, so she said. 'Yes,' giving him a brilliant smile. 'Is that going to be a problem?'

'Not with me,' Alistair said, grinning. 'I like powerful women.'

Lisa laughed. 'I wouldn't say powerful was quite the right word,' she said, flexing the muscles in her arm, the smile still on her face.

'Oh, I think the word suits you admirably.' James's

sarcasm fell between the couple, like a weight, throwing them off balance.

Alistair looked surprised. James was such a gentleman, and kind. He had never heard his friend speak to anyone like that before.

Lisa's expression tightened with the effort required to control her anger. 'Really,' she said, her private-school English accent in sharp contrast to James's Scottish burr.

It aggravated him, and his grey eyes darkened to the colour of the sea in winter.

Lisa was delighted. Words and their tone were weapons she was expert at using. But even as she smiled, part of her was drawn to the passion she knew linked her with this man, and, try as she would, she could not quell a longing to be crushed in his arms—not taken, but crushed—crushed against his strong body, feel every part of him close to her, so close that only the heat of their bodies would lie between them.

James saw the quickened desire in her eyes and it swept away his anger. She wanted him, and it was his turn to smile. He would not admit to himself that the light shining on her hair made it appear fairer, nor that he longed to run his fingers through it before grasping a handful of it so that he could pull her face close to his, so close that only their breath would whisper between them before he kissed those soft pink lucious lips until the coldness left her eyes and they became languid like a summer's day.

James's mouth became dry as he fought to pull himself together. These feelings were purely chemical anyway. She was a cold-eyed, autocratic English b——

The phone rang to interrupt his thoughts. It was Janet telling him that the theatre was ready.

'Will you give the anaesthetic, Alistair?' James was

walking towards the door. 'I'll tell you about the case as we go.'

'Fine. I was knocking off for lunch anyway,' Alistair said in a dry tone.

James grinned. 'Knowing what a devoted doctor you are, I knew you wouldn't mind. Anyway, you're getting too fat.' Which was not so. Alistair had a lean, tough frame which he kept in peak condition. He was a member of the mountain rescue team.

James ignored Lisa. They had the door open when Alistair said, 'Won't you need an assistant?' He smiled at Lisa as he spoke and it warmed the cold anger she felt at James's dismissal of her.

'Miss Halliman is not employed by this hospital.' James's tone was stiff.

'She'll only be assisting.' Alistair smiled. 'Anyway, it's in Kevin's best interest, isn't it?' He was unaware that he was using the same words that Lisa had, but James remembered. Alistair glanced at the blonde woman. 'Do you have surgical experience?'

'Yes.' She did not tell him, and indirectly James, that she was a fellow of the Royal College of Surgeons.

'Well, in that case, you'll be able to assist,' said James.

Lisa heard the coolness in his tone, but ignored it and just said, 'Yes.' Then added, 'I take it that you are qualified to perform such intricate surgery?' knowing it would infuriate him.

James had to clench his teeth to stop himself screaming abuse at her. No one had ever treated him with such impudence before — no one would have dared.

Alistair's eyes had rounded at Lisa's presumption.

'James was one of the youngest to get his FRCS,' he spoke up in defence of his wordless friend. 'He's a brilliant surgeon.'

Lisa was quite enjoying baiting James. 'Really?' she

said, raising her eyebrows. 'What is he doing here in this backwater, then? Surely his talents are wasted.' Lisa had spoken as if James were not there — ignored him as he had ignored her.

James was not goaded into telling her his reasons. Let her think what she liked, but a dangerous light entered his eyes.

Alistair had often wondered himself why James was, as Lisa said, 'wasting' his talents and was disappointed when James did not enlighten them.

James gestured for Lisa to precede him, without a word, but every line of his body was taut.

She did not feel as if she had won a victory, but swept before him with her head held high.

Having seen the treatment-room, Lisa wondered what the theatre would be like. She was surprised to find that it was well-equipped, well-lit and compact.

Alistair left them to prepare his young patient. The scrub-room was not as modern as the theatre, but it was adequate. There were two small changing cubicles.

Lisa went into one of them and changed into the theatre greens she found lying on a seat. The trousers were too big and long. She wondered if they were James's and managed to keep them up by tying the front into a knot. The bottoms she turned up.

The V-necked top was also too big for her; it kept slipping off one shoulder, but this did not worry her. The sterile gown would keep it on. Rapidly she plaited her hair into one long plait and fixed it round her head like a halo.

'I've left a pair of the theatre sister's boots for you. I expect they'll fit.' James's voice came through the curtain.

'Thanks.' The small consideration galled her. She wanted nothing from him. Then she grinned. Except his body, she thought. I bet he looks marvellous in theatre greens. She stepped from the cubicle and slipped on the boots.

James was scrubbing up at the sink. He straightened to look at her and was unable to hide his amusement at the change from smart, svelte female with glorious hair into this waif-like creature dressed in his hand-me-downs. She looked vulnerable and he felt his hatred vanish.

'I should have given you some of Janet's greens,' he said softly.

'That's all right, I managed,' and she smiled, suddenly glad her hatred had disappeared.

James did not only look marvellous in his theatre greens, he looked magnificent, and she felt her skin burn. His hat covered his hair and was pulled down far enough to hide his stitches.

Lisa tucked her hair into a theatre cap and turned on the elbow taps, avoiding his eyes. Simultaneously they pushed backwards through the doors, their arms held well away from their clothes. A nurse hurried foward to assist them into their theatre masks and gowns.

As Lisa stood opposite to James across the body of the small child, she thought she had never seen such an attractive pair of eyes. There had been Roger, a surgeon with whom she had had an affair, but he could not compare with James. She smiled.

James saw the smile in her eyes and supposed it was a 'Now let's see what you can do' smile. He was secure in his own ability and did not need to prove himself to her or anyone. So why did his gloved hand tremble slightly as he held it out to Janet for the first instrument, after Alistair had given him a nod to signify that the child was ready? He did not want to impress this Lisa Halliman, did he?

But Lisa was impressed—impressed to find that there

was equipment to deal with microsurgery, and that James was an expert in that field.

James worked on the tiny finger with a delicateness and precision a watchmaker would have envied. He did not hurry, but worked steadily and without hesitation. What a waste, thought Lisa. James glanced up at her, and something of what she was thinking must have shown in her eyes, those beautiful blue eyes which were looking at him with such seriousness and not a bit like Charles Halliman's. James looked down and concentrated on Kevin's finger, sighing to himself.

Lisa's assistance was without fault and James forgot, for a moment, that she was not his usual colleague standing across the table from him. It was only as he glanced up and saw that it was not Janet, who usually assisted him, but this tall, slim woman who aggravated him so.

Lisa was enjoying working with James so much that it was not until they had finished and she glanced up at the theatre sister who had pulled down her mask that she saw it was Janet Cameron. Did this woman do every job in the hospital?

James noticed Lisa's surprise. 'Janet is the best nurse I have ever known.' He put his arm round the Matron, who blushed.

'Och, away, Jamie.' She gave him a push, but she was pleased. 'I'll take the wee one now if Alistair and yourself are satisfied with him?'

Alistair pulled down his mask and smiled. 'He's all yours.'

'I'll be down to see how he is as soon as I've changed,' promised James.

Janet nodded. The 'dirty' nurse had brought in the trolley. She had removed her gown and was dressed in the yellow of the auxiliary nurse; she was about forty. A few strands of grey lightened the brown of her hair.

The prettiness of her youth was fading and her brown eyes had a tired look about them.

Was the matron the only trained nurse in the hospital? Lisa wondered in astonishment.

There was only one shower in the changing-room. A subtle difference in their attitude towards each other, occasioned by her admiration for his skill as a surgeon and her competence in assisting him, had removed the last trace of acrimony between them.

At that moment, James saw Lisa not as Charles Halliman's daughter, but as a respected professional; and she saw him not as a man who had caused her heartache, but as the best surgeon she had ever encountered.

'Thomas's?' he asked.

Lisa grinned. 'How did you know that was my hospital?'

What a difference that grin made to her face, thought James. She looked younger, especially with that plait around her head.

'Oh, it was just a guess.' He smiled.

This time Lisa's heart ached, not with pain, but with longing.

'Going to share the shower?' he challenged with a mischievous grin.

'OK.'

For a moment he was nonplussed. He had been so sure she would refuse.

Lisa laughed at his surprise. 'I'm a liberated woman,' she said, more brightly than she felt. If only he had not challenged her; she could never resist a dare.

'You'll find a towelling gown in your cubicle,' he said, grinning.

Lisa nodded. She could hear the water running in the shower as she stripped, and a vision of James's naked body standing with the water flowing over his body inflamed her desire. She did not know if she would be able to cope in the shower. Then, suddenly, she did not care. She only knew that she wanted him, wanted him so much that she felt her breathing stop.

Taking a big gulp of air, Lisa left the cubicle and threw back the shower curtain, dropping her robe as she did so. She could have cried when she found the shower was empty. Then she was furious. It had been a tease, and she had fallen for it. Damn the man.

Lisa turned the shower to cold. The icy water felt like needles drumming into her, but it swept the desire from her body.

She was dressed and combing her hair when James returned. He could hear the swish of the brush.

'Sorry to have deserted you,' he said and he sounded regretful. 'But the nurse came just as I'd turned on the shower.'

Lisa pulled the curtain aside, the brush in her hand. 'Was it Kevin?' she asked in concern.

'No. It was a patient I operated on yesterday — an appendicectomy.' His face was serious. 'It was very inflamed and we just caught it in time. If she had had to wait for the ferry or the air ambulance it would have burst.' He frowned. 'She's on intravenous fluids and her arm was becoming red. I transferred the drip to the other arm.'

James was speaking as one surgeon to another. Lisa suddenly realised that he was not blaming her for the imminent closure of the hospital any more, and an exciting idea entered her head. It would need careful thought before it was voiced, but what a challenge.

James took the sudden brightening of her eye to signify professional interest and he smiled.

I do wish he wouldn't smile like that, Lisa thought. It does terrible things to me.

The antagonism that James had felt since meeting

Lisa — was it only yesterday? It felt like a lifetime — was softening. He had seen her kindness to Kirsty and he liked this side of her and, even though she had assisted him just once, he felt they could work well together.

Then he had an idea. Perhaps if she was part of the hospital she might feel like supporting him in his fight to keep it open. Perhaps she might finance improvements, so he said, 'How would you like a job? I could influence the Highland Health Board in your favour. Alistair's leaving at the end of April and going to Canada.'

He was actually serious, Lisa thought. 'You don't know anything about me,' she said, playing with the brush in her hand. 'Apart. . .' she smiled wryly '. . .from my being Charles Halliman's daughter.'

He made a dismissive gesture. 'You did quite a good job on me.' He touched his forehead. 'And you proved yourself to be an able assistant in surgery.'

'But what about the general practice side of it?' She had to admit that his offer appealed to her.

'Well, you could do your general practice training.' He grinned. 'An intelligent woman like yourself. . .' he splayed his hands '. . .will soon pick it up.'

'I thought Scotsmen were hard-headed businessmen.' She smiled at his flattery.

'Well, not many doctors want to live on an island, and for an Englishwoman you're not a bad doctor.' His grin showed her it was not meant as an insult.

Lisa laughed. 'You're that desperate?'

James's laughter was his reply.

'I'll need to think about it,' she said, though she already knew she would accept. Then she frowned. 'But if the hospital's closing. . .'

'I mean to fight it,' he said, his face grim.

Lisa sensed his desperation and, suddenly, she wanted to help this man. His dedication was the same as her own, but she did not want him discussing the closure now, not until she had worked out in her own mind how the idea she had thought of would work, so to lead him away from this line of conversation she said, 'How's the head?'

'Fine. No headaches, no nausea, no blurring of vision.'

'Do you want me to take the stitches out when the time comes?'

'No. Janet will do it.'

Lisa detected disappointment behind the words and wondered what she had said to cause it.

James was disappointed. He had hoped for an immediate acceptance, a commitment.

'But to get back to my offer,' he persisted, his manner professional. The humorous rapport between them had cooled on his part. 'I'd like to know as soon as possible.'

'Will tomorrow be soon enough?' she asked drily, disappointed herself at his withdrawal. Why should I bother? she asked herself. What is it to me if the hospital closes? It's not as if James would not be employed. He would still have his general practice. Why should I help him? She was a stranger and English, and he was a difficult, infuriating man. But a man, a small voice inside her said. The only man who has stirred you to a passion you know lies waiting, that just needs a touch to ignite.

But that was not the only reason for her to stay. She had been restless for some time. Her job as a surgical registrar had been satisfying, but her application for a junior consultancy had not been successful and this had depressed her. The lawyer's letter had acted as a stimulant. She had resigned her post on an impulse, and here she was, and here she would stay. James McKinnon was not going to move her.

'Yes,' he said, turning away.

Her answer would not be yes, he was sure, and felt a relief that puzzled him. Why should what Charles Halliman's daughter did affect him?

Lisa collected her bag.

James was in the shower as she left.

CHAPTER FIVE

NEXT morning, Lisa knew she would find James in his surgery, which was opposite the matron's office. Alistair's room was next door.

There were already patients waiting in the reception area. They were not, as Lisa had supposed yesterday, casualties or outpatients. They were just waiting to see the GP.

She had arrived at eight o'clock to make sure of seeing James before he started work.

'Is Dr McKinnon in his surgery?' she asked Moira.

'He was called out to a maternity case at six this morning.' Moira glanced up at the clock. 'He should be back any minute.' She crossed to a board of keys, selected one and handed it to Lisa. 'Why don't you wait in his surgery?'

Lisa found it difficult to adjust to the familiarity everyone used towards James. She wondered if the patients would call her Dr Lisa, if James had not changed his mind about taking her on as trainee.

She looked round his surgery curiously. The room was as spartan as the flat upstairs. There was a large old-fashioned desk to the right of the door. A picture frame, with its back towards her, was the only thing of a personal nature. It stood beside a sphygmomanometer, an auroscope and an opthalmoscope. A pile of case-notes for the morning surgery were waiting in the centre.

A substantial chair, its brown leather seating cracked with age, was behind the desk. An old eye-testing chart hung on the cream wall. A leather examination couch stood on wooden legs below it, and a weighing machine was close by, its white paint flaking.

The whole room looked as if it had not changed since the Thirties. And yet there was something comfortable about it. It wasn't a sterile room, like some Lisa had entered, all white and glossy.

Lisa could imagine the dramas that had taken place here over the years, but they had not left a discordant atmosphere. There was nothing threatening in this room, though it did fill her with sudden apprehension. Was she capable of dispensing kindness — the kindness that seemed to pervade this room? Was she?

She stared at the back of the picture on the desk with troubled eyes, and had picked it up when James came in.

Startled, and feeling guilty, she almost dropped it. He came forward and took it from her, turning it to face her.

'*My Lady Love*,' he said.

His words brought a sudden ache to her heart. Then she looked at the picture and was unwilling to admit to the relief the photograph of a sailing boat gave her.

'*My Lady Love*?' she queried.

James grinned. Lisa was looking particularly attractive. Her hair was twisted into two buns and fixed at the back of her head with hairpins, but the severity of the style did not make her look older. It drew attention to her high forehead and the fineness of her bones. There was nothing waif-like about her today, though. Her light grey suit with its straight skirt and excellent cut fitted her figure to perfection. Her white jumper was plain, but of soft cashmere. Her black court shoes were of a serviceable height, and the black shoulder-bag was leather and unfussy. She looked like an executive. Not quite the doctor the islanders were used to, and James hid his doubt behind a smile. Maybe his idea of involving her in the hospital had not been such a good one, but he would have to proceed now that he had asked her to take over from Alistair.

'Yes, that's its name,' he said as he set it back on the desk and put his doctor's bag down on the chair with a thump. 'The love of my life,' he said, grinning.

Then his face straightened. 'Well, what's the verdict?'

The light from the window caught half of him, shadowing the rest. It was almost as if there were two men — the one with the stitched forehead and the other without. He was wearing an old tweed jacket the colour of the mountains — grey, blue, mauve. It looked as if it would retain its shape when he took it off. His trousers were grey, as was his tie. His shirt was white, and Lisa had a vision of him against a background of heather, his head held up to the sky. He was part of this land as she would never be. It was not in her blood, and a sadness swept over her, a sadness she could not quite understand. Why should she feel like this? she wondered. She had only met him two days ago, though it felt like forever. She was not in love with him. How could she be? She doubted if she was capable of love.

James did not see the sadness in her eyes. He saw what he thought was doubt. Ah, I was right, she's going to refuse, he told himself with some relief, so he was surprised when she said, 'I'd like to accept your offer, but I've little obstetric experience.'

'Hmm.' James looked at her thoughtfully. 'A little practice will help that and we have a very good district nurse-midwife. We're not often called in.'

'But you've just come from an obstetric case, haven't you? Moira mentioned it.'

He grinned. 'Well, not directly. I shaved first.' Then he became serious. 'It was a retained placenta, Annie MacIntosh. It was her third child and complications weren't expected.' He splayed his hands. 'But there you are. A helicopter took her to the mainland hospital.'

Lisa frowned. 'Well, surely, that proves the health authority's case.'

James was furious. 'No, it certainly does not. If this place were properly equipped, Annie could have been treated here.'

Lisa did not want to argue, so she said, 'Yes, I see.'

James looked at her with suspicion. She seemed to have given in too easily.

Lisa was suddenly remembering why she had decided obstetrics was not for her. Too much emotion was involved. There was the father's anxiety and the mother's apprehension. Then there was the joy. Lisa could not cope with the couples' joy, and when things did not go right she was equally uneasy. That was why she had chosen to become a surgeon.

She should tell James right now, but how could she? He had respect for her as a surgeon and she did not want to lose that.

James looked at his watch. 'Time to start work.'

There was a second chair in the room beside the one for the patient and he lifted it forward. 'You'd better get used to GP work right away and sit in.'

'Thanks,' she said drily.

James pressed a buzzer, and a few moments later there was a knock on the door. 'Come in,' he said.

He had given Lisa the notes of the first patient to read. Mrs Ida Maxwell was a woman of sixty with almost white hair and the anxious face of the constant worrier. She and her husband ran a grocery shop in the town and their son toured the island with a grocery van.

'Good morning, Ida.' James smiled. 'Do you mind if Dr Halliman stays?'

'Er — no.' Ida Maxwell's anxiety was so great that she

only had eyes for Dr Jamie. She did not even see the slender woman until he mentioned her.

Lisa glanced at the notes. Ida seldom visited the doctor and was apologetic about disturbing him now.

'I'm sorry to bother you, but I got such a fright.' Her forehead wrinkled with anxiety.

'How can I help?' James's voice was gentle.

'The dog sleeps in our room. If he wants out in the night, he paws my side of the bed.' She took a deep breath. 'Last night, he woke me up and I rose, but oh, I felt so dizzy and sick. The dizziness passed, but the sickness didn't and I'm frightened. I have to be fit to help in the shop.' She was close to tears.

James smiled reassuringly. 'We'll just take your blood-pressure,' he said, rising with the sphygmomanometer in his hand. 'You've had your blood-pressure taken before, haven't you?' Ida nodded. After he had finished, he said, 'Well, that's fine,' giving her a smile. 'Now I want you to follow my finger with your eyes.'

Ida's hands tightened in her lap, but she did as he had requested.

James went back to his seat. The movement of his hand as it crossed the paper recording his findings was the only sound in the room. A splatter or two of rain splashed the window-pane as he laid aside his pen and looked at Ida with a smile.

'There's nothing to worry about,' he said. 'All that happened was that you got up too quickly from a deep sleep and your blood-pressure dropped. That's what made you fell dizzy and sick.' He smiled. 'That's all it was. Everything's fine now.'

'But I still feel sick,' Ida said, her anxiety only partly relieved.

'A good night's sleep will take care of that. Try to remember not to jump out of bed, but to rise slowly.'

'Thank you, Dr Jamie.' The anxiety lifted from her face. 'Thank you very much.'

James went with her to the door. 'You'll be fine now.' His voice was confident.

Lisa saw Ida's shoulders relax, and she envied James's ability to communicate so effectively. She thought again that she should not have accepted the post.

The rest of the patients consisted of minor cases — a child with a sore throat, a joiner whose injured thumb was healed and who had come for a signing-off note, a man needing a medical for an insurance firm. They all looked at Lisa with curiosity. They all knew who she was.

She did not realise how hard she had been concentrating until James said, 'Coffee time, I think,' and found she was tired.

She followed him from the surgery to a small staff-room further down the corridor. They were the only ones there. An electric kettle stood on a table beside some mugs, sugar, coffee and a pint of milk. James filled the kettle from a small sink.

The click of the switch as he turned it on made Lisa jump. She had not been aware of how tense she was until then and she hoped James had not noticed. He had, but made no comment.

Lisa watched as he put coffee into the mugs. No logos on these ones, she thought, as she saw that he remembered she liked it black. This impressed her more than she liked. He was a dangerous man and she should be on her guard against the attraction he had for her.

James was out to impress her. He had told her he would fight for his hospital and if this meant wooing Charles Halliman's daughter he would do it. He was a canny man and little courtesies, he knew, meant a lot to a woman.

Handing her a mug, he offered biscuits from a box. She took one, although she did not eat biscuits.

'Drink up,' James said. 'We've half a dozen visits to get through before lunch.' As she set down her empty mug, he added, 'I don't think that skirt is quite suitable.'

This annoyed Lisa, who was feeling uneasy anyway. The surgery this morning had been different from what she was used to and she was having unaccustomed doubts as to her ability. Normally her confidence was supreme. So she frowned.

'What's wrong with it?'

'You'll see,' was all he said, but there was a twinkle in his eye.

And so she did when he took her outside. The Range Rover she had noticed when she had arrived was to be their transport.

'We can take my car,' she said hastily, viewing the green boots in the back with distaste, and wondering if he did veterinary work as well. A big black Labrador's sleepy head reared up at the window. It was sitting on the seat she presumed was for her.

Lisa stepped back a pace.

'Rory won't hurt you,' James said, smiling in amusement.

'Oh, really?' She did not move. 'He looks awfully big.'

'Don't worry, you won't have to share the seat with him.' James opened the passenger door and Rory clambered out, much to Lisa's relief.

She lifted an old blanket the dog had been lying on between finger and thumb and looked at James with distaste.

'Throw it in the back,' he said. 'It's easy to see you're a city girl.'

This put her at a disadvantage, and she was more

disadvantaged as she looked at the high step. She would have to hitch her skirt up above her knees to climb in and even then——

James laughed, and before Lisa could protest he had swept her up into his arms and put her, none too gently, on to the passenger seat. His face was so close to hers that she could smell his aftershave.

'Next time wear trousers or a full skirt,' he said.

Lisa could hear the laughter in his voice and mentally ground her teeth.

'I'll do that,' she said, forcing a light laugh. She composed her face and waited for him to join her.

Her attempt to present a calm elegance was foiled when James called, 'Come on, boy,' and Rory leapt into the back of the Range Rover and gave Lisa a big lick on the side of her face.

'Oh, good, he likes you,' James said, trying to hide a smile as he glanced at the now dishevelled young woman beside him. Rory had knocked the pins from her hair, dislodging one of her buns.

Lisa's face was stiff with fright.

'Oh, come now.' His tone was mocking. 'No need to look so disapproving.'

'I'm frightened of dogs,' she whispered. It was shock that had made her tell him, and as soon as she had spoken she regretted it.

Ever since her father had rejected her and her mother could not be bothered with her, Lisa had concealed her feelings. To have exposed them now, and to this aggravating man, left her feeling vulnerable. She clutched her shoulder-bag to her chest.

James had the engine running, but turned it off and looked at her. 'You should have told me,' he said gently. 'I would never have let Rory. . .' There was amusement in his eyes as he added, 'Kiss you. I'll reserve that pleasure for myself.' James grinned.

Lisa smiled. He was going to open his door when she said, 'No.' She was not going to let him think her a wimp. 'I'll get used to him.'

She did not see the admiring glance James gave her; she was looking straight ahead, her head up, her bag still clutched to her chest.

'I hope you do,' James said, turning on the ignition, 'because he's a very good watchdog, for all his daftness, and won't let anyone near the Range Rover.'

Lisa thought about his words as they drove through the town and went in the direction of her house.

'Surely you don't need protection on Bruig?' she eventually said.

'We do have the occasional drug addict, especially during the holiday season.'

'Yes. I hadn't thought of that.'

'Would you like to change into something more comfortable?' James asked as they neared the turn-off for her house.

'Yes, please.' She smiled her appreciation.

The battered Range Rover looked out of place parked in front of Halliman House.

'Do you mind if Rory had a run about?' James asked as the dog leapt out after them and sat at his master's feet.

'No.' Lisa preferred the dog to be outside rather than in the house.

Jean had heard the Range Rover and opened the door to greet them. 'Dr Jamie.' The pleasure in her eyes was unmistakable. She opened the door wider. 'Shall I bring some coffee, Miss Lisa?'

Lisa looked enquiringly at James.

'We don't really have the time,' he said. 'We've only come for. . .' He paused slightly before he added with a hint of mockery, 'Miss Lisa to change.'

They stepped into the house and Jean showed James into the lounge.

Lisa had not brought many clothes with her. She had kept on her London flat. This visit to Bruig had been meant as a holiday to give her time to think about her future plans. She only had one pair of trousers in her suitcase, put in, like the tweed skirt, as an afterthought; they were navy blue corduroy, rather like the ones James had been wearing when she had first met him. She was forced to team this with a thick cable-knit sweater as her white jumper and blue leather jacket would be unsuitable.

I wonder if he expects me to wear trainers? she thought with amusement, slipping her feet into flat slip-ons. She did not bother with a bag, but she did plait her hair and fix it in a coil at the nape of her neck.

'You'll have to dress quicker than that when you're on call,' James said when she appeared, his face breaking into a grin when he saw her outfit.

Lisa had expected him to make some remark about her clothes, even suggesting that his father should employ her instead of himself, but his comment was unjust. She had taken under ten minutes to change.

'I bet you couldn't change any more quickly.' Her eyes were angry.

'Perhaps we should find out,' he said, his grin broadening.

He was teasing, but she accepted the challenge. 'Any time you like.'

He laughed. 'It's a date.' He could not hide the desire that sprang into his eyes. The navy blue sweater and corduroys outlined her figure, and the colour made her eyes seem bluer. She was a beautiful woman.

'Come on.' He reached out his hand. She would have to take it. It would look ridiculous if she didn't, but she did not want to. His touch, however fleeting, excited her.

With her hand in his, they were in the hall when James called, 'The mistress will be out to lunch, Jeannie.' The mockery was back in his voice and Lisa blushed.

Jean appeared at the front door as James was calling his dog. 'You'll be home for dinner though, Miss Lisa?' she asked.

'I certainly will.' Lisa smiled as she stood back for Rory to jump in.

'We're popping in to see Kathy McLachlan first,' James said as he looked to left and right at the end of the drive.

The road followed the coast for quite a while. The silence in the Range Rover was broken by the engine's noise and the dog licking his paws.

Lisa was glad James did not speak. She did not want to be distracted. Her eyes were on the sea. Its greyness beneath the almost white sky seemed to go on forever. It looked like a massive sheet of slate that could be walked upon. There was no wind to disturb its smoothness, no land in the distance to break the skyline, no bird to give it life. It seemed to call to the bleakness deep inside her and she shivered.

'You need something more than a jumper to keep you warm.' He had mistaken the reason for her shiver. 'Early April can be cold here. I'd offer you the dog's blanket,' he teased, 'but I don't think he'd like it.'

Lisa grinned. 'I wouldn't dream of upsetting Rory.'

Hearing his name, Rory reared up, put his paws on the back of her seat and licked her face.

'Down, Rory,' James commanded, seeing Lisa's face tighten. 'Sorry about that, but you've only yourself to blame. You shouldn't be so delicious. I wouldn't mind a taste myself.' James was surprised to hear himself make such a remark. It wasn't like him to be facetious.

They turned on to a track on the right. The land either side of them stretched to the hills. The biscuit colour of the moorland grass was mixed with grey. Sheep, their thick coats making the heads look smaller, cropped incessantly.

'Wild flowers will give it more interest soon,' James said.

A farmhouse came into view. 'Kathy had her first baby four days ago.' He glanced at Lisa, expecting a comment on the inadvisability of having a first baby at home, but when she did not speak he said, 'Kathy wanted the baby to be born at home, wanted it to be part of the farm, and Margaret Kerr and I allowed it.' He sounded defensive. 'Kathy's antenatal period was uneventful and we were both there for the birth in case of complications.'

He parked the car. 'Stay, Rory,' James commanded as they climbed out. He took Lisa round to the back of the Range Rover. 'You'd better see this,' he said, opening the boot.

He opened a large box. Inside, intravenous sets, bags of IV fluids, syringes, needles, dressing packs, splints, bandages, equipment for stitching wounds and other useful things were stored. Another box held blankets. Lisa was impressed and surprised.

'Alistair and I are on call for the mountain rescue team and for accidents or anything else.' He grinned. 'We're the flying squad.'

Lisa laughed. It was the first genuine laugh James had heard. It softened her face, made her look younger, and James had a sudden desire to touch her.

How on earth am I going to manage as part of the mountain rescue team? Lisa wondered, suddenly longing for her comfortable London flat and all that that city could offer. I must have been mad to accept James's challenge, and he must have been made to make it. I'm quite out of place here.

And even more out of place Lisa felt as they were taken up to Kathy's bedroom by her mother.

'The baby's fine,' said Sally Stewart with a wide smile for her daughter.

Lisa's heart ached with envy at the obvious rapport between Kathy and her mother.

'Thanks for everything, Dr Jamie,' Kathy said, including Lisa, whom James had introduced, in her smile.

Mrs Stewart took the baby from her daughter and put it in its cot. She then turned down the bedclothes for James to feel Kathy's uterus.

'That seems to be fine,' he said, 'but Margaret will be in to keep an eye on you. I'll just take a look at the baby.'

'Allan's thrilled with it being a boy,' Kathy said. 'Girls are not much help with the heavy work on a farm.'

The baby lay contentedly as James checked the umbilical stump. His fingers were feather-light in their gentleness and his expression had softened.

Anguish caught at Lisa's heart. Had her father ever looked at her like that?

James glanced up at her. The bleakness had left Lisa's eyes, but the memory of it lingered, leaving them cold. Had he let his obsession with keeping the hospital open outweigh his judgement? Genuine kindness and understanding were essential in a GP. This woman could be kind, as he had observed with Kirsty, but had it been an impersonal kindness? A GP needed to give more than that.

Lisa saw the smile for the baby leave James's face as he looked at her, and knew it was because of the expression in her eyes. She had seen it happen before, but how could she explain? Then anger caught at her. Why should she?

The smile was back on James's face when he turned back to Kathy. 'That's fine. Just keep the stump dry using the medi-swabs Sister Margaret gave you. Don't hesitate to call us if there should be any bleeding.'

'Thanks, Dr Jamie, and you too, Dr Halliman.'

James was silent as they climbed back into the Range Rover. Rory gave Lisa another kiss, and this time she did not stiffen. In fact, she welcomed this sign of affection and stroked his head.

Her gesture broke the tension between herself and James. 'Rory gets round everybody in the end,' he said, pleased that Lisa had overcome her fear of the dog so quickly.

They left the farm and continued up the road away from the direction from which they had come. The land was as bleak as her heart. The sky had become overcast and the clouds shadowed the moorland with black patches.

They drove round a bend in the road and the sea was before them once more. A few pines sheltered a whitewashed croft which stood alone.

The loneliness of the white croft suddenly reminded James of his first sight of Lisa as she had stood waiting for the ferry. There had been a loneliness about her which he only now realised.

He took a quick glance at her. The sky had darkened the interior of the Range Rover, so that her face and blonde hair stood out above her dark clothes. It had a remote, withdrawn expression, and compassion softened his eyes. Fine doctor he was. Only too ready to find fault with her because she was the daughter of Charles Halliman; only too eager to take advantage of her if he could. She was vulnerable, this girl, and he was ashamed of himself.

Lisa glanced at his profile and thought that she was the reason for his stern expression, but changed her mind when he smiled and said, 'You'll like Mrs Innes; she is one of the old crofters. She originally came here from the Shetlands and knits beautiful gossamer scarves.' He smiled gently. 'She's blind now, but it doesn't stop her knitting. I think it's because it's part of her and she's been doing it for so long that she doesn't need to see. She has a twin sister who looks after her.'

James parked the Range Rover and allowed Rory to jump out. 'There aren't any sheep here,' he explained. As they approached the croft, he said, 'Sheena's daughter wanted them both to live with her in the town, but Sheena won't budge and May agrees with her. I don't blame them.' Lisa saw compassion in his face as he glanced at her. 'Their memories live in this house.' It was something that had struck him about Halliman House. There had been no photographs, no evidence of anybody having lived there. 'They married brothers when they were seventeen. Sheena's children, all six of them, were born here. Her husband and May's were lost at sea. They were fishermen.'

James looked towards the sea; his profile was thoughtful.

'My father, as a young man, was on the boat at the time. He was the only one saved.' Now why was he telling her this? He had not told any other woman of his acquaintance. 'I visit every fortnight to see that they're all right.' He paused, and then added as if to himself, 'Perhaps it's because I feel guilty because my father's alive while their husbands are dead.'

'Perhaps that's the reason,' Lisa said quietly, 'and perhaps not. We can't take the blame for what our parents do, or for what happens to them.' She raised her head proudly. 'Nor should others blame us,' she said firmly.

She was right, thought James, hearing the reprimand in her voice. He should not hold her responsible for Charles Halliman's lack of interest in the hospital. Just because she had a likeness to her father did not mean that she was a clone of him, and he resolved to see her as she was — see her for herself, a beautiful, attractive, intelligent woman.

There was a silence between them broken only by the sound of a gull. Lisa saw a subtle change in his face. It lost the wariness that had been behind it since they had first met, and he smiled that wonderful smile that soothed and bathed her heart. She smiled in return and a faint blush warmed her cheeks. Even her blonde hair seemed brighter. It was like the sun rising in a blue sky that was tinged with pink.

She looked like a different person, James thought. Or was it just that he was seeing her differently? It was a pity to break the moment, but there were patients to see.

'Come,' he said, holding out his hand.

The hand she put into his was cold and he wanted to warm it and put it, with his, into his trouser pocket. He wished he could warm the coldness he felt within her as easily.

He grinned, and, suddenly, she was happy, and it was as if her happiness was reflected in the sky. A breeze blew the black clouds towards the hills, and a blueness tinged the almost white sky.

Lisa wished she could hold this moment forever, but the loudness of his knock on the door swept it away. Her hand slipped from his pocket as they entered.

'It's only me, Jamie,' James called.

'Come away in,' Sheena said.

James opened a door to the right of the tiny hall and

stepped into a living-room. It could not be called a lounge, for it had a far more lived-in appearance. Photographs were crowded everywhere — mantelpiece, bookcase, table, windowsills and hanging on the walls. There were big photographs and small ones, in silver and wooden frames. The room was alive with the past.

A fireguard protected a peat fire. A frail woman, dressed in black with a white shawl about her shoulders, made to rise.

'No, no,' James insisted. He placed a hand on her shoulder to prevent her.

'But you've brought someone with you, Jamie.' The soft Highland voice matched the gentle, lined face. The blind eyes were blue, and must have been as pretty as Lisa's when she had smiled at James.

James picked up Sheena's knitting, which had fallen to the floor, and put it back into her hands, patting them as he did so. She caught hold of his hand and drew it to her face.

'You're so good to me, Jamie,' she said.

Lisa would have thought that he would be embarrassed by the gesture, but he was touched by it.

'I've brought Miss Halliman to see you,' he said affectionately, 'or, rather——' he smiled at Lisa '—I should say Dr Halliman.'

Dishes clattered in the kitchen extension attached to the living-room. 'Would you tell May you're here, please, Jamie? She's getting deafer by the day.' Sheena shook her head in a resigned way.

As James went into the kitchen, Sheena held out her hand. Lisa took it and Sheena put her other one over it.

'Come nearer the fire, Dr Halliman. You won't be used to our cold climate yet.' She smiled gently, and although Lisa knew the old lady was blind she had a strange feeling that Sheena saw more than Lisa would have wished.

She could hear James laughing in the kitchen and wished he would come back into the living-room. Sheena's intentness was making her nervous.

'I hope the peace of this island will help you,' Sheena said. 'Soothe your troubled heart.' The words fell quietly.

'Thank you,' Lisa said simply, and was glad when May, with James carrying a tray, came in at that moment. She knew about the feyness of the Celts and did not want to hear any prophesies.

James introduced Lisa to Sheena's sister, who was identical, except that May was more practical.

'Set the tray down here, please, Jamie,' she said, pushing the photographs to the back of the table. The fragile china clinked as James put the tray down. 'I hope you like tea, Dr Halliman,' she added, glancing in Lisa's direction.

'Yes, thank you.' Lisa accepted the flowered cup and saucer. 'Call me Lisa,' she said with a smile.

James brought a chair for her. She loved his politeness.

'Oh, we couldn't do that,' the twins said in unison. 'It wouldn't be respectful,' unconsciously repeating Jean Fraser's words.

'Dr Lisa, then.'

'Yes.' Both sisters smiled.

Lisa was impressed at the way May managed to pour the tea with her arthritic hands. Her hips, and probably other joints, must be affected too, she thought. She had noticed how slowly May had walked and observed the deep lines of pain between her brows.

Lisa and James did not stay long. Rory was given a drink of water before he climbed on to the back seat.

As they drove away, Lisa said, 'What treatment is May having?'

James told her the drugs, then said, 'She refuses to have a replacement hip operation. Said she couldn't leave her sister alone.'

'But couldn't Sheena have gone to live with her daughter while May went into hospital?'

'Sheena doesn't know about May's arthritis. If she did, she would insist that they both left the croft.'

'But wouldn't that be better if they moved into the town where help is so near?'

'Didn't you hear me when I told you that their memories are in that house?' He glanced sideways at her, his face frowning at what he supposed was her lack of understanding.

'Yes, I heard you,' she said sharply. 'But if May should fall and break a leg, what would happen to Sheena?' she persisted. 'It's all very well being sentimental, but it wouldn't help either of them in a situation like that.'

James's face relaxed. 'You're right, of course, but the postman, Margaret Kerr, meals-on-wheels. . .' Lisa's eyebrows rose in surprise. 'Yes. We do have such a service, and all those people watch over them. Then there's Sheena's daughter who phones every day at a certain time, and if she doesn't get a reply she comes out immediately.'

'Yes.' Lisa still looked doubtful. 'But what about the winter?'

'Yes. That does worry us, but we just have to hope for the best.'

How marvellous to have people who cared so much. Lisa's heart ached.

'An island community is knit more tightly than that of other places, especially here, where we can be cut off by the weather. We have to be self-sufficient.' His voice was serious. 'And we have to be able to rely on each other.'

Was he wondering if she, a city girl, would be good enough? She glanced at his profile. His expression was bland, so she assumed it was not doubt on his part, but well-meant advice.

Their next patient also lived in a croft, but a considerably extended and renovated one. It overlooked the next bay where a small community clustered near by.

'Ben Anderson,' James said, as they left the Range Rover, 'brought his wife, Shirley, and young family here from Edinburgh fifteen years ago to escape the rat-race.' He clipped the lead on to Rory's collar. 'They have created a cottage industry. Ben was a business manager and has the expertise. His wife designs unusual sweaters. She spins the wool herself and dyes it to the colour she wants. Local women are employed to knit her patterns and she pays them a decent wage.'

'You approve of this.' It was not a question, just a statement.

'I approve of anyone or anything that will help the island's economy.'

'You love this island, don't you?' she said softly.

They had been walking towards the croft. James stopped. Rory reared up to put his paws on his master's chest. James looked over the dog's head at the picturesque white crofts grouped together like sheep for comfort. The clouds had returned, but they were not black and threatening, but white and woolly. A strip of pale, almost white sand edged the bay.

'I wish I could paint,' James said in almost a whisper. 'Yes, I love the island. It's part of me.'

He was standing sideways to her, his strong face etched sharply against the sky. The profile he presented did not show the stitches on his forehead. A slight breeze lifted his black hair and she saw strands of grey among its darkness. The heather colours of his clothes made him appear not just part of the island, but rooted in its earth. Strength was there in the way he held himself—proudly, aware of his heritage and the stronger for it.

Lisa almost felt insignificant beside him and all that he represented, but she had risen above her unhappy childhood using only her strength of will and determination not to let anything conquer her. She straightened her back. She knew she was as good as he was.

Though, as she stood beside this man, she was loath to admit that she lacked something. And then, with an indescribable anguish, she knew what it was—warmth. James commanded affection. She had seen it in the eyes of all those whom she had met. She had no place here. Was there anywhere she did have a place?

James sighed a sigh of contentment. He looked down at the woman beside him, and never knew afterwards whether it was compassion for the bleakness he saw in her eyes or something deeper that stirred him—that made him pull her roughly into his arms, hold her close and stroke her hair.

He tipped her face up to the sky. A gull flying over at that moment was reflected in their blueness. He did not see shock or surprise in their depth, just an eagerness.

His lips came down upon hers in a kiss that was more gentle than the tightness with which he held her, and her cold heart warmed and expanded with an emotion she was not yet prepared to recognise.

Her response was almost desperate and it was he who had to part them.

'This is not quite the time,' he murmured, his voice rough with emotion.

She cried, in her anguish, and without thought, 'Will there be a time?'

What had he done? James was shocked at her intensity and involuntarily said, 'Yes, there'll be a time,' to give her the reassurance she wanted.

He put his arm about her shoulders and she hers about his waist as they walked towards the croft, but he was disturbed. Was he prepared to make a place for this unusual woman in his heart?

The Andersons greeted them as if James and Lisa were a couple. Shirley had seen the kiss from the croft's window and had rushed to tell her husband who was sitting at his desk in the part of the extension that was converted into an office. Ben had fractured his leg a week ago while out on a mountain rescue exercise and had had to live with jokes about the rescuer being rescued ever since.

'Now then, Shirley,' Ben said in a patient voice. 'You mustn't read a wedding into a kiss.' He smiled in a resigned way. His wife was an incurable romantic and had tried, more than once, to matchmake for James.

Lisa's face was pink with the warmth of James's kiss as he introduced her. She immediately liked Shirley and her husband and greeted them with a smile that lacked her usual wariness.

James was disconcerted at seeing this. Lisa looked like a woman in love and he confined their visit to just checking that Ben's toes were pink and that he was exercising them.

'You must stay for coffee,' Shirley insisted.

'We've still more visits to do,' James said, edging Lisa towards the door.

'Oh.' Shirley looked disappointed.

'Lisa will stay next time, won't you?' He smiled at the blonde girl.

'Yes, I'd love to,' Lisa said, her spontaneity surprising herself. Surely a few words that held a promise had not broken down her protective barrier? And yet she felt more relaxed than she could ever remember.

'You must both come for dinner soon,' Shirley said as she saw them out with a smile.

Lisa was feeling uncomfortable. It was obvious from Shirley's manner that she had seen the kiss. Lisa was also appalled at having read more into the kiss than it warranted and of having exposed her desperate longing for affection to James. It had never happened with anyone before, and had only happened now, she told herself, because she was so attracted to him. That she had fallen in love with him never entered her head.

James was very quiet in the Range Rover and Lisa sensed that she was the cause. He was probably regretting his impulsive gesture, made, she was certain, out of kindness.

Lisa wished that she could creep into a hole with her embarrassment. This was something new to her. So, taking a grip on herself and raising her chin, she said with a light laugh, 'I hope you didn't read too much into my response to your kiss.'

She was voicing exactly what James had thought she was feeling about him. He should have been relieved that his gesture had not been taken seriously, and he was — wasn't he?

'It's just that I'm sex-starved.' Her words, spoken jestingly, broke into his thoughts.

'Well, I'll be happy to do something about that,' he said, laughing, and the awkward moment passed.

CHAPTER SIX

LIGHT breezes blew April into May. The relationship between James and Lisa developed into friendship. The kiss, even though it had not led to anything intimate between them, had released Lisa. It was wonderful to be able to communicate easily and without stiffness with the patients.

The more she treated them, the more she realised how important the hospital was for emergencies and casualties. The sudden collapse of Janet Cameron towards the end of May further drew attention to their lack of facilities.

Lisa was taking morning surgery when Janet came in without knocking. This was so unlike the matron's strictly professional attitude that Lisa looked up in surprise from prescribing penicillin for little Ian Duffy's sore throat.

'He'll be better in a day or two after you start the penicillin. Give him the syrup four times a day and make sure you finish the bottle, even if he seems better.' She smiled to soften the firmness of her instruction.

'Yes, Doctor. Thanks.' The red-headed young woman lifted her three-year-old son from her knee and put him down. 'Don't touch that,' she admonished the child, who was about to grab the small vase of daffodils on Lisa's desk. 'Oh, he does lead me a dance,' she said, but with a grin.

Lisa was looking at Janet's anxious eyes and noticing the whiteness of the older woman's face and her breathlessness.

'You won't need to come again unless he becomes worse,' Lisa said to Mrs Duffy as she walked them to the door. 'Don't hesitate to call me if you're worried.'

As she closed the door on Mrs Duffy's thanks, Lisa looked with a professional eye at Janet.

'I think you had better lie down.' Lisa gestured towards the couch.

Janet did so without question and this alarmed Lisa further. The relationship between the two women had remained cool and professional, but not friendly. Janet must be really frightened to have come to her. Why hadn't she gone to James who was next door?

Perspiration had broken out on Matron's brow and she was still breathless. Lisa removed the cap and undid the silver buckle. She also undid the collar.

Janet's face was tight with pain. 'The pain came on just as I reached the top of the stairs,' she said, her usual firm voice a whisper. 'I've never had it before.'

Lisa was taking Janet's pulse — it was slightly raised. She gave the anxious woman a reassuring smile as she rolled up the navy blue sleeve to apply the cuff of the blood-pressure machine on to Janet's upper arm.

The lines of pain were receding on the white face as Lisa took Janet's blood-pressure. It was about normal for a woman of her age.

'The pain's gone now,' said Janet and went to sit up.

Lisa pushed her back gently. 'Just rest. I'll get James to have a look at you.'

Janet caught hold of Lisa's wrist. 'No. You examine me.' She was blushing. 'I'd be embarrassed with Jamie. He's like a son.'

'All right.' Lisa did not want to upset Janet by insisting. She did not want to agitate her.

Janet undid the buttons of her dress, sat up and slipped it down to her waist. Lisa settled the ear-pieces of her stethoscope comfortably in her ears and listened to Janet's heart sounds. What she heard confirmed her diagnosis.

'I'm sure you don't need me to tell you what's wrong,' Lisa said with a smile. 'You've had an attack of angina.'

Janet was fastening her dress buttons. 'Yes,' she said, looking up at the blonde doctor. 'At first I thought it was a coronary.' Anxiety flared in her eyes again. 'But I knew when the tightness went away so quickly that it was probably angina.'

Lisa always had a carafe of water and a glass in her surgery. She filled the glass and handed it to her patient. Janet drank. As Lisa removed the glass, the matron smiled. 'Thank you.' Her head fell back on the pillow. 'My mouth was so dry.'

'I'd like you to rest for a bit,' Lisa said. 'I'd like to take some blood for cholesterol among other things.' She smiled wryly. Janet would know exactly what tests the doctor would order. She glanced at her watch. 'We might just catch the ferry.' Any blood samples had to be taken to the mainland hospital for analysis. Important results were phoned through to Bruig. 'And you'll need a coronary arteriography, which, as you know, means a catheter has to be inserted into the brachial artery and slipped into the aorta, eventually reaching the coronary artery when radio-opaque fluid is injected and X-rays taken.'

Lisa knew what Janet would say before the matron said, with a frown, 'That means I'll have to leave the island.'

'I'm afraid so.' Lisa brought the tray of syringes, needles and bottles for various blood samples, and put it on a small table beside the couch. 'You know we can only take routine X-rays here. Anything as specialised as this has to be done on the mainland.' She smiled sympathetically. 'Do you have anyone who can go with you?' Lisa knew nothing about Janet's circumstances. She did not even know where she lived.

'No, but I'll be all right,' Janet said hastily.

Lisa was just filling in the details on the blood forms when a knock on the door was followed by James coming in.

'Oh, sorry. Moira said you didn't have a patient.' Then, as he came further into the room, he saw past the curtain Lisa had only partially drawn round her patient.

'Janet!' he said, concern sharpening his voice. He was beside her in a moment, his fingers on her pulse, his eyes assessing her professionally.

Lisa joined him. 'Janet has had an attack of angina,' she said quietly.

'Are you sure?' James frowned at Lisa. 'You should have called me.' His tone was aggrieved.

'I would have,' Lisa said in a cool voice, 'if I had been unsure of my diagnosis.' She was annoyed at his implied lack of faith in her ability. 'I was going to tell you.' It was her turn to sound aggrieved.

James took Lisa by the arm and led her over to the window. 'Did you consider that Janet might have had a coronary?' he said in a voice low enough for Janet not to hear.

Lisa suppressed her rising anger with difficulty. Seeing his anxious expression and the paleness of his face, except for the scar on his forehead that had reddened, helped. She suspected that part of his anger was because he was hurt that Janet had not come to him.

'Yes, I did,' she said as evenly as she could. 'The substernal pain came on after exercise; Janet had climbed the stairs. It subsided quickly when she lay down.' Lisa smiled as she added, 'Janet diagnosed herself.'

'And you accepted her diagnosis?' James's tone was

sharp with disbelief. His face tightened with anger. 'Did you take her blood-pressure and pulse?'

This was too much. He was treating her like a medical student. Any consideration for how he was feeling vanished. Lisa was furious.

'Because I don't have your expertise as a general practitioner doesn't mean that I can't tell the difference between an attack of angina and a coronary thrombosis.' She spoke in a precise way. 'Janet's blood-pressure had not dropped, her pulse was rapid, she was not showing signs of shock and the pain passed quickly. If she had had a coronary, the pain would still be there, her blood-pressure would be low and her pulse rapid. She would be in shock. Wouldn't that be so?' Her tone was sarcastic.

James rubbed a hand across his forehead. 'Yes,' he said. He looked out of the window, but he could not see his beloved mountains from which he drew his strength. The window looked on to a yard.

Taking a deep breath, he turned back to Lisa. 'I'm sorry. I should not have doubted you. You're a fine doctor.' The anger had left his face, but the anxiety remained. 'It's just that Janet means a lot to me. She was the district nurse, midwife and health visitor on the island when I was a boy and she nursed my mother.' His eyes clouded. 'She died of cancer when I was twelve.' He glanced towards the couch. 'It was Janet's devotion to her job that influenced me into becoming a doctor. She's a fine woman and excellent at her job.'

Lisa's anger left her. His compliment regarding her ability had thrilled her, but it was the vulnerability that she saw in his face and his confiding in her that had swept it away.

'We'd better go and see her or she'll be suspicious if we linger,' Lisa said. 'Probably will think her condition is worse than it is.'

'Thanks for understanding,' James said with a smile.

They crossed over to Janet and stood side by side. James smiled down at the face looking affectionately up at him. 'Looks as if you'll need a few days off,' he said.

Janet made to sit up. 'I'm fine now,' she said.

James pressed her back on to the pillow. 'You've been doing too much.'

'But I must work.' Janet was looking anxious again. 'I'm too young to retire.'

'You're to take a fortnight off.' James's voice was firm. 'And you are not to do any more theatre work. We'll employ a theatre sister who can help on the wards as well.'

James expected Janet to protest vehemently, but she didn't. She just said, 'I've got just the person for you. My niece. You remember her. She came to stay with me last year.' Janet's eyes were bright. 'She's an excellent theatre sister and an all-round nurse as well.'

James frowned. Then his face cleared. 'You mean that gorgeous brunette you introduced me to?' His eyes smiled. 'Yes, I do remember her.'

'Well, she was telling me in a letter I received yesterday that she was looking for a job. She's just come back from Australia.'

'Weren't her parents overseas a lot? Her father was in the Foreign Office, wasn't he?'

Mentioning the Foreign Office should have warned Lisa, but it didn't.

'Yes,' said Janet. 'Would you like me to contact her?'

'Yes.' James thought for a moment. 'She should be told about your angina anyway. It sounds as if she would suit us very well and I'll certainly tell the Health Board so.' There was a gleam of interest in his eyes that Lisa did not like. She was jealous and mad at herself for being so. How well did James know Janet's niece? 'It would be company for you as well,' James was saying as Lisa fought with her jealousy.

'It would be nice,' Janet said. Then after a pause she added, with a resigned note in her voice. 'But I don't know if she would want to stay here. She might feel cut off.'

James patted her shoulder. 'Phone her and see,' he said kindly.

'I've only got her post-box number.'

'Then write.' James smiled. 'But not today. Today you rest. I'll take you to your flat.' He grinned. 'I don't trust you to go there yourself — you might slip back into your office.'

'I'll cover for you,' Lisa told James as she helped Janet off the couch.

'That won't be necessary,' James said. 'Janet stays in the flat opposite to mine. I'll just tell Moira.'

'Come with us, Dr Lisa.' Janet never called Lisa by just her Christian name. 'It is your coffee time. You and Jamie could have it in my flat.'

Lisa was not surprised to find that Janet lived in the hospital. The matron's work meant everything to her.

'No, thanks,' Lisa said gently. 'You go with James.' She crossed to the desk and wrote out a prescription. 'Glyceril trinitrate,' she said with a smile. 'There's no need to tell you to pop one under your tongue if you get the pain again.'

James took the prescription and glanced at it. 'Are you sure you're a doctor? Your writing's too neat.' He was grinning. His little joke took the tension from the room. 'I'll visit you this evening to make sure you're comfortable,' Lisa promised Janet.

'I can do that,' said James.

'No.' Janet's voice was firm. 'Dr Lisa is my doctor.' Then, seeing the hurt in James's eyes, she said gently,

'You're like a son to me,' and her face flushed. 'I find it less embarrassing having a female doctor.'

James glanced at Lisa. 'You know, I never thought of that. I wonder if that was why Mrs Farino asked to see you instead of me?'

'Well, I don't want to crush your ego, but yes, that is why.' Lisa grinned. 'We do have our uses, you know.'

'So that's why she agreed to have a pelvic floor repair.' He smiled. 'I've been trying to persuade her to have the operation for ages. I don't think she had time or the energy to do the postnatal exercises with six children and the chip shop to help in, and as a result her pelvis floor muscles are slack and she's troubled with incontinence.'

Lisa liked the way James was not annoyed at her success. He was generous of spirit, more generous than she probably would have been. She liked to be right. She would have smiled stiffly in his place. Or had she changed?

After they had left, Lisa saw another patient — a man with the beginnings of a leg ulcer. She prescribed an antibiotic dressing and advised him on how to apply it. 'Come back in a week's time, or earlier if you're worried,' she told him.

As the door closed behind him, Lisa leaned back in her chair. They could do with a practice nurse, then Mr Wilkie could have had his dressing done properly, here, at the surgery. She was worried that his superficial ulcer would become worse. He was sixty-six and lived alone.

Lisa went along to the small staffroom and was making herself a mug of coffee, still thinking of Mr Wilkie, when James came in.

'Thank you,' he said.

Lisa blushed. She presumed he was thanking her for her professional care of Janet, but said, nevertheless, 'What for?'

'For being kind.'

His reply was so different from what she had been thinking that it silenced her. She had never thought of herself as being kind, for she had often been accused of being ruthless.

'Kind?' She voiced her surprise eventually.

'Yes, kind.' James came closer. 'You are, you know.' He smiled down at her with affection. 'You've changed since you came here. Didn't you know?'

The tone of his voice was so gentle that she felt herself being drawn to him. It had been difficult, since that kiss, to look upon James impersonally. Although she had laughed it off at the time, her dreams were full of longing. She had to admit that James was meaning more to her as day followed day. But she was an expert at hiding her emotions, unless taken unawares, and was glad about that now, for she could smile and say a simple, 'Thanks.'

She took a drink of coffee so that she would not have to say any more, but she blushed afresh because she knew his eyes were still upon her.

'I would like to talk to you, James.' She glanced up at him and wished she hadn't. He was looking particularly attractive this morning. His face was well-shaven, his black hair had been recently cut and he did not look as tired as she had sometimes seen him.

Taking a deep breath to steady her fluttering heart, she said, 'Are you free to dine at Halliman House this evening?'

'Yes.' James gave her a quizzical look. 'Not going to tell me you're resigning, are you?'

She laughed. 'Good gracious, no.'

'Going to show me what keeps you so occupied that you refuse my invitations?' His tone was teasing.

Lisa grinned. 'Perhaps.'

He took a step closer to her. 'What time?' It was

true, James thought. She had changed. Her blue eyes had lost that icy look. They were as soft as the blue cashmere jumper she was wearing. She was looking particularly attractive this morning, her face devoid of make-up, looking fresh and clean.

'You've done your hair in a different way,' he said softly.

Lisa laughed to hide the quickening of her heart. 'I've worn it in a chignon for the past week.'

He grinned 'Is that what. . .' he touched the coil lightly '. . .you call this?'

His nearness was making her so nervous that she almost dodged backwards as he touched her hair.

'I prefer your hair down,' he said, pulling out the pins so that it fell about her shoulders. His voice had roughened.

His sudden action excited Lisa so that she longed to touch him, but she remained motionless, her rounded eyes upon his face as he ran the silken strands of her hair through his fingers.

His hand was so close that she had an unbearable longing to rest her cheek upon it. The longing must have shown in her eyes for his fingers stilled and his hand caught the back of her head and pulled it close, his eyes holding hers until her face was just a breath away from his.

His lips when they met hers were warm and demanding and she responded with an urgency she found difficult to restrain. His hand moved down her back, setting her skin alive. Her arms went round his neck as he pressed her tightly to him. His desire was as strong as hers, his urgency as great.

While part of him was afraid of crushing her softness, his arousal was so great that he was swept higher and higher until he felt he was losing his control and would be unable to stop. He would have had the clothes off them both if Lisa had not prevented him. He was appalled at the strength of his passion.

'This is not the time.' She tore her lips from his, unconsciously using his words spoken at their last kiss. Saying them recalled that time.

James swallowed. 'You're right.' His voice was unsteady. He took a deep breath, straightened his tie and ran his fingers through his hair. 'Perhaps this evening?' His eyes were still heavy with desire.

'Perhaps.' Her voice was just a whisper.

Lisa pulled down her jumper, which his searching hands had disarranged and said, in a voice that was not quite steady, 'Would you like some coffee?'

He gave a laugh. 'Hot, sweet and strong?'

Lisa glanced sideways at him, smiling at his joke. Her face was still flushed, her eyes languid. Only by making a supreme effort was James able to stop himself reaching for her again. Then his tense face relaxed.

'What time tonight?' he said.

'Eight o'clock,' she said, as she handed him his coffee.

Lisa knew, as James did, that the attraction between them that had been building since they had met must be satisfied. They could no longer see each other every day, feel the underlying tension, without something happening.

James finished his coffee. 'I'll bring the wine,' he said, setting his mug down. 'See you later.' He smiled and was gone.

As the door closed behind him Lisa sat down before her legs gave way and drank some coffee. There had been something different about that kiss. It had held a passion that frightened yet exhilarated her. It threatened to lift her to a height never before reached with Roger and she was afraid that she would not be able to control it — that it would control her.

Lisa stilled a threatened shiver. She reached for the phone on the table beside her and dialled her number to tell Jean that a guest was expected for dinner.

Before she left for home she called in to see Janet and was pleased to find her patient looking more relaxed.

'I didn't thank you,' Janet said as she opened the door of her flat. Her smile had lost the stiffness it had usually had when she had greeted Lisa on previous occasions.

The flat was basically the same as James's, but there was a marked difference between the two. Janet had made hers a home. The walls were freshly painted a magnolia colour. The curtains in the lounge were floral and matched the suite. The carpet was green and the furniture teak.

'Will you have enough room for your niece?' Lisa spoke as if Janet's niece were already a member of the staff.

'Yes. The flat has two bedrooms.'

Janet lifted a silver photograph frame from the mantelpiece and handed it to Lisa, saying with pride in her voice, 'This is my niece.'

It showed Janet with her arm through that of a young, pretty, dark-haired woman, with the sea as a background.

Lisa looked at the younger woman with interest. She wanted to see what James had found so attractive, but what she saw filled her with shock.

It was a good photograph, sharp and clear. There could be no mistake. The young woman smiling back at her was Karen Carmichael — the Karen Carmichael who had betrayed her.

CHAPTER SEVEN

THAT evening Lisa's fingers trembled as she fastened
the buttons on her pink silk blouse, but they were not
shaking because her thoughts were of James and of
what the evening might hold. It was Janet's photograph
of her niece that caused them to tremble.

She pulled on a black crêpe skirt; her legs were
encased in black tights and she slipped her feet into
black patent leather court shoes.

She sat down in front of the dressing-table and
gripped its edge. She hardly recognised the pinched,
pale face that stared back at her from the mirror. Her
hair was loose about her shoulders and she knew she
should do something about it, but felt too disheartened
to bother. She just kept staring, and eventually her face
in the mirror disappeared and the scene of Karen's
betrayal took its place.

It was an operating theatre. Lisa was performing her
first appendicectomy. The house surgeon was assisting.
Karen was the theatre sister.

It was a straightforward operation, but there had
been a fair amount of bleeding and quite a few swabs
had been used.

The senior registrar came in. He was an attractive
man and Karen was having an affair with him. Lisa had
remonstrated with her about it in the corridor just
before the operation.

'You know he's married?' she said.

'Oh, yes,' Karen replied airily. 'So what?'

'I just don't want you to get hurt,' Lisa said.

They had been at the same expensive boarding-school. It was there that the friendship had been formed. Karen was vivacious, attractive and fun to be with. Lisa wished that she could be so easygoing.

'I won't be the one to get hurt,' Karen said, smiling, but the smile did not reach her eyes.

It was the first time that Lisa had noticed hardness in her friend's voice.

She's playing with him, Lisa realised, and immediately squashed the critical thought. She was very fond of Karen and did not want to see faults in her friend. Anyway, didn't *she* use men? But it was a rule with Lisa that she did not go out with married men, and if she thought a man she was seeing was becoming too fond of her she broke off the relationship.

The senior registrar stood beside Karen and a whispered conversation with little spurts of laughter ensued. The registrar left just before Lisa was about to finish.

Karen had sent the nurses to lunch. This was the last case of the morning's list and they were running late. Lisa had been counting the swabs she had used. Before closing the wound, she said, 'Swab count, please,'

'Oh — er — ' Karen stuttered, then told her.

'Are you sure?' Lisa asked.

'Of course,' Karen replied sharply.

Lisa was tense. The whispered conversation in the background had added to this tension, agitating her, so that she doubted her own count and accepted Karen's word.

'Very well,' she said and closed the wound.

The patient was just about to be removed from Theatre when the houseman, who was inclined to be timid, swallowed and said, 'I think the sister's wrong. I think there's a swab missing.'

Lisa believed him.

'Bring the patient back,' she said, and attracted the attention of the anaesthetist. 'We'll open her up.'

'What?' Karen's tone was aggressive.

'You heard,' Lisa said in a hard voice. 'We're opening this patient up. I'm sure that a swab has been left inside.' Any affection she had had for Karen was gone and its place was taken by heartache for the loss.

'I protest,' Karen blustered, but Lisa ignored her and went to scrub.

Yet she could not help but hope as she opened the wound that she was wrong. Karen had been her friend since they were six years old.

But she was not wrong. Lisa removed the swab and closed the wound. The theatre had been silent throughout. The nurses came back at that moment just as Lisa finished.

She went with the patient to the ward and had her monitored very closely. The woman made a good recovery, but there was to be no recovery where the friendship was concerned.

When Lisa returned to the theatre, Karen was clearing up. She did not apologise and there was no guilt on her face.

Lisa recalled incidents from the past which she had suppressed, not wanting to believe them. How Karen had lied at school about her parents, saying her father was an ambassador when he had only been a very junior member of the Foreign Office. How, when they were older, Karen had slipped out of school to meet a boy and had persuaded Lisa to lie by telling their housemistress, who checked the dormitory before lights out, that Karen was in the toilet. There were other things too. Little things that had left an unpleasantness, but which Lisa had pushed out of her mind, chiding herself for her disloyalty.

But this was different. A patient's life could have been forfeit.

'You are responsible for the swab count,' Lisa said. 'You were too busy with your. . .' her lips curled '. . .boyfriend to take proper care.'

'Ha!' Karen's eyes widened. 'So that's it. You're jealous because Richard prefers me.'

Lisa was stunned into silence.

'Just because you suffer from. . .' Karen pulled a face '. . .heartache. . .' she used a little girl's voice for the word '. . .it's made you bitter.' There was a sneer on her face. 'You can't love. It's not in you.'

For a moment Lisa was stricken. Then she realised what Karen was doing. By attacking, Karen was hoping to draw Lisa's attention from the missing swab.

Heartbroken as she was, Lisa was not to be fooled. Her head came up.

'But I do care what happens to my patients,' she said coldly. There was no hate in her eyes, just disgust.

When Karen saw that her ploy had not had the effect she had hoped for, she said, 'Well, that timid house surgeon won't tell, and I'm sure you won't either. As for the anaesthetist. . .' she spread her hands '. . .he's an old flame of mine.' There was supreme confidence in her tone.

Lisa turned without a word and left the theatre. That had been four years ago and she had not seen or heard of Karen since.

Now she was coming here. The vision of the theatre scene vanished and Lisa's face appeared, once more, in the mirror with the bedroom reflected behind it.

What I need is a stiff drink, she thought as she rose.

She was on her way down the stairs when the bell rang. James! She had forgotten he was coming.

'I'll answer it,' she called, just as the bell went again.

As the door swung wide, James said, patting the

walls, 'I thought, with this thickness, that you mightn't have heard my ring.'

'The electrics are pretty efficient,' said Lisa with a smile.

The excitement she had felt in the staffroom had faded. All she could think about was Karen. Everywhere she looked she saw Karen's face superimposed. Even as she greeted James and joked with him, it was Karen's face that looked at her.

As the evening progressed, James sensed Lisa's withdrawal. She seemed bright enough, but there was no expectancy about her and her eyes — she seemed to be hiding behind them.

The meal was excellent. 'This rainbow trout is very good.'

'Thank you,' Lisa said, with a smile.

She had suggested to Jean that candles on the table might make the room look less austere. She sat at the head with James on her right. The candlelight shadowed the rest of the room, creating an island at the top of the table.

The wine she had drunk with the meal had relaxed her and pushed Karen's apparition into the background, but, even though she could now concentrate on James, the other woman's presence lurked in the shadows.

Their conversation had consisted of generalities during the meal. Jean had removed their empty sweet plates and as Lisa pushed the cheese-board towards him James caught hold of her hand and said, 'Was there a special reason for this dinner or. . .?' He gave her an intense look, his eyes darkening with desire. She was so beautiful sitting there with the candlelight softening her features. The pink blouse gave a reflected warmth to her pale skin. This was not the efficient doctor, but a desirable woman sitting beside him. Something was disturbing her, though. Perhaps she was regretting her reaction to him in the staffroom?

James felt a sharp stab of disappointment. He wanted to take her in his arms — wanted to kiss her withdrawal away — wanted — wanted. He had to take firm control of himself, and he was helped in this by Lisa pulling her hand away.

'Yes,' she said, finding it difficult to ignore the expression in his eyes. Wrapping her professional cloak about her, she said, 'I wanted to discuss the hospital with you.'

James leaned back in his chair, leaving the cheese-board untouched. His eyes narrowed, his expression became defensive. Her words had acted like a cold shower, dampening his desire.

Lisa laughed and cut herself a piece of Brie.

'I'm not going to criticise your beloved hospital,' she said after taking a mouthful.

'Oh?' His expression was still cautious.

Lisa took a sip of wine.

'Well?' His voice was impatient.

'Did you know that you have great big frown lines between your eyebrows when you're mad? If you don't do something about them you'll end up looking an awfully cross, grumpy old man.'

She was teasing him and he relaxed.

'I need a good woman to smooth the lines away each night, preferably in bed.' He smiled mischievously as he added, 'Perhaps Janet's niece would do the job.'

Lisa had been feeling light-hearted until he mentioned Karen. It brought her presence out of her shadows. Lisa's face tightened.

James thought the sudden change in her was due to jealousy. The relationship between himself and Lisa was delicate. He wasn't sure himself what the outcome would be, but he did not want to spoil what they had.

It was like a bud about to flower, so he said, with laughter in his eyes, 'I was only teasing.'

'I'm not jealous,' she said, her eyebrows rising at his assumption.

The tone with which James said, 'Oh?' implied that he did not believe her, but Lisa could not explain about Karen, so she changed the subject and said, 'I was wondering what you would think about turning this house into a hospital.'

James was so astonished that he was speechless for a moment. Then his eyes gleamed with excitement. He didn't say, Are you kidding? or, Don't be stupid. He just said, 'Would it be big enough?'

Lisa smiled, pleased with his reaction and, leaving her chair, held out her hand. 'Come and see.'

James had no thoughts of pulling her into his arms as he took her hand in his. His mind was racing. What possibilities this would open up. He had difficulty in controlling his excitement.

As they toured the house, they vied with each other.

'We could convert this. . .'

'We could have the operating theatres here. . .'

'This would make a good ward.'

James's enthusiasm was infectious. Suggestions flew from one to the other. By the time they had returned to the lounge the coffee Jean had left for them was cold.

'We haven't seen the kitchen yet,' said Lisa gaily, lifting the tray.

James grinned. 'So we haven't.'

Jean was taking a packet of mince out of the freezer as they came in. 'I'll make you some fresh,' she said, smiling at the handsome couple. Noting their excitement, she wondered if there was more than professional interest between the two.

'Thanks,' Lisa said.

They continued their discussion as they made their way back to the lounge where a fire had warmed the room. The coffee, when it came, was most welcome.

'It will cost a great deal of money to transform this house into a hospital,' James said.

'I know.' Lisa smiled. 'My father left me a great deal of money and there's all this.' She gestured towards the furniture and ornaments.

'But don't they have sentimental value?' It sounded extreme to James.

'No,' she answered shortly. 'My parents were divorced when I was eight. I only saw my father twice after that, and both times he made it quite plain that I had to make my own way.' She did not realise how vulnerable she looked. 'He told me he would put me through university and give me an allowance. After that. . .' she shrugged '. . .I never saw him again. My mother found me a nuisance and sent me to boarding-school. I had plenty of money from her, but. . .'

So that was why he sensed a desperation to be loved. He reached forward and took her hand. This time she did not pull it away.

'His will came as a complete shock.' His hand tightened on hers. 'I was only in this house once and that was the time my parents separated.'

Lisa did not want to explain further. She did not want to feel that dreadful heartache again. 'So you see. . .' she gave him a brittle smile that wrenched at his heart '. . .this house has unhappy memories, and nothing in it matters. I would like you to go with me to the lawyers where arrangements can be made for a trust fund or whatever is needed to ensure the success of this scheme. We'll need to consult the local authorities as well. We don't want it to be a private nursing home, do we?'

James shook his head emphatically, more to shake away the longing to take her into his arms and kiss away her sorrow than in answer to her question. He had forgotten how he had planned her involvement in the hospital so that she would use her money to its advantage. He wanted her as a doctor and as a lover.

'We'll have to see what they say. I also thought it would be a good idea if we could encourage the islands nearest to us to send their patients here. You have the surgical expertise,' she said.

James's eyes blazed with zeal. 'I returned to the island because I was disillusioned with the health service — all those long waiting lists that never seemed to become shorter.' His face became serious. 'I owe you an apology.' His voice had softened. 'I thought you were just a rich, uncaring woman when you arrived, but you're not.'

Wasn't she? Was this hospital idea of hers genuine? Or had she suggested it so that James would think well of her? Was she trying to buy love?

No, a voice inside her cried. You're not like Karen. She wished she could beg James not to encourage the employment of Janet's niece. Perhaps Karen would not accept the offer. The island would be too quiet for her.

'Why so troubled?' He touched her face gently.

Lisa longed for the comfort of his arms, longed to rest her head on his chest, longed for the security his strength could give her.

Her eyes were vulnerable and sad, and James knew, instinctively, that all she wanted, at that moment, was warmth, the warmth another human being could give.

He pulled her into his arms and stroked her hair and felt her tense body relax against him. James suspected that Lisa did not lower her guard very often and he felt flattered, and something more. Was it love? Or was it gratitude for her generosity? Whatever it was, just the feel of her softness in his arms roused his desire.

Lisa felt his breathing quicken, his arms tighten, and, raising her face to his, saw the wanting in his eyes.

'James.' His name slipped from her lips. All thoughts of the new hospital, all thoughts of Karen vanished as if they had never been as she was swept by a fierce yearning that was more than a longing for comfort.

James searched her eyes and, seeing there a desire as strong as his own, kissed her. It ignited a passion that just kissing would not satisfy. Jean had popped in earlier to say that she was going to bed, but it would not have mattered if she had still been up and might have disturbed them. They were lost to everything but each other's needs.

The soft white rug in front of the fire was their bed, the warmth from the fire's glow their blanket. Only the table lamps were lit. They cast the shadow of their lovemaking on to the ceiling so that there appeared a ghostly couple as well as themselves writhing in a passionate frenzy.

James's touch inflamed her and Lisa's response roused him to a passion he had not known he possessed. He was glad she was not a virgin for he would not have been able to control himself. He had never before made love to someone whose passion equalled his own.

'Lisa, Lisa,' he whispered, his mouth close to hers. He wanted to tell her how wonderful she was, but words were not enough.

Lisa reached up and pulled his head down, her mouth searching for his. Again and yet again their passion reached its peak until exhaustion made them fall apart, and even then their fingers stayed entwined.

There did not seem any need for words. It was all there in their eyes — a languid satisfaction.

The fire had lost its brightness. It was almost as if its glow had been stolen by the couple whose skin held its rosy colour.

Lisa shivered and sat up, but James would not release her hand and pulled her down on top of him. She smiled a lover's smile and her lips were just about to touch his when a small chiming clock struck one.

'Perhaps I should go,' he whispered with her lips touching his.

'Perhaps.' She smiled. 'Or perhaps you would like to stay the night?'

'No perhaps about it.' He grinned. 'But it wouldn't do your reputation any good. The old values still hold on Bruig. A wedding-ring is a must for a couple to sleep together.'

For a moment, Lisa wondered if James thought like that, then dismissed it. He was too sophisticated.

They rose and gathered up their clothes. Lisa did not even remember shedding them; her whole being had been lost to James.

They crept to the front door hand in hand, smiling.

'See you tomorrow,' James whispered.

Lisa could not bear to let go of his hand so that their arms stretched out, as he moved away, until their fingers slid along each other's as he left her.

The two rear lights of his car stared back at her like angry red eyes. A dreadful desolation enveloped her as they vanished from sight. It was worse than heartache — it was more than heartache, for before she had not been in love.

CHAPTER EIGHT

STILL hot from James's touch, Lisa found it difficult to view their recent lovemaking impersonally, but knew that she must. She had never been in love before and now that she was she felt she must be especially careful. The day her parents had decided to divorce was burnt into her brain. The acrimony—the hate still lingered in this house. Lisa shivered.

She went back into the lounge to tidy up, but no matter how she tried to distance herself from what had taken place here she only had to look at the rug to feel James's touch, feel his lips on hers.

I'll have to get rid of that rug, she thought, as she collected the coffee-tray and took it through to the kitchen.

Upstairs, Lisa went and had a shower, but the hot water did not wash away the heat in her body, so she ruthlessly turned on the cold, gasping at the shock. This did help.

That night, James coloured her dreams so that she woke with a languid smile on her face which she quickly banished. She must not let her emotions rule her or her longing for true love. Did James love her? She did not know.

As she washed and dressed next morning, her mother's cry of, 'I only married you for your money,' insidiously slithered out of her memory like a snake. Was James more interested in what her money could do for his dream?

Try as she would, she could not help herself from looking for his car when she arrived at the hospital.

Could not stop herself from listening for his voice as she approached Reception. She left her surgery door ajar before calling the first patient so that she might hear his footsteps.

I must stop this, she told herself and rose abruptly, so abruptly that she knocked her knee on the desk. She was rubbing it when James came in.

'I hope I'm not responsible for that bruise,' he said with an intimate smile.

His self-satisfied grin did the trick. It steadied the sudden race of her heart. James's 'That's my little woman' look was enough to put the steel back into her melting bones.

Lisa's expression was cool as she said, 'No, I just banged my knee on the desk.'

James was bewildered and a little hurt. Was this cold person the woman who had shown such passion last night? Had he done something to upset her? Or had she been using him?

The smile left his face. He had thought she was joking when she had said, that first time he had kissed her, that she was sex-starved, but perhaps. . .

'I must start my surgery.' Her words interrupted his thoughts.

'So must I.' His expressionless face hid his disappointment. He had thought there had been something deeper than mere sex between them last night. Maybe his original estimation of her had been correct.

Lisa sat down abruptly as the door closed behind him, but even though he had left she could still see his face—how it had stiffened at her coolness. Part of her cried bitter tears, but the other part firmed its resolve. She had no proof that last night had been anything more than an inevitable coming together of a strong physical attraction on his part. Lisa had risen above her parents' rejection, but she did not think she would be strong enough to face James's rejection if she confessed her love. She felt it would destroy her.

It was unfortunate that she had to call James in for advice concerning her first patient. She had hoped that she would not have to see him so soon, but she lacked experience where medical cases were concerned. Lisa was worried that the reason for Patrick Casey's loss of weight was due to something other than alcoholism.

Looking at his notes, she said, 'I see you missed your last parentrovite injection.' She glanced up at the patient. He was in his late fifties with a gaunt face and dark hair that was streaked with grey. It was long and needed cutting. His clothes looked as if they had been slept in and Lisa suspected that they had. She had seen quite a few like Mr Casey sleeping rough on the Embankment in London, and had patched up quite a few in Casualty after fights.

'This vitamin injection is very important.' Lisa's tone was firm, but gentle.

Patrick stared defiantly at her, but his hands were twisting. 'I forgot.' His voice was gruff, but he seemed lethargic. Then he coughed.

'Hmm.' Lisa looked at his notes again. There was no mention of chest trouble.

'Have you had that cough long?' she asked.

Patrick looked at her. His blue eyes were watery, his skin dry and pale. He was one of the lost ones and Lisa was sorry for him.

'Yes,' he said. It seemed to take all his energy to answer.

Lisa picked her stethoscope up from the desk. 'I'd like to listen to your chest,' she said, leaving her chair.

She helped him remove his top clothes, which were not very clean. He sat with his shoulders bowed as if he did not care what happened to him. His ribcage showed through the thinness of his skin.

He shivered. 'I'll be as quick as I can,' Lisa said, warming the bell of her stethoscope in her hands before placing it on his back.

The frown lines between her brows deepened as she listened. 'Take a deep breath,' she said.

Patrick did and coughed.

When Lisa had finished, she helped him to dress, then took out her thermometer.

'It's just a bit of bronchitis,' Patrick said in a strong Irish accent. 'Are you going to give me the injection now?' He seemed eager to leave and ran his tongue over his dry lips.

'I want to take your temperature first.'

Patrick frowned, but did not object when she put the thermometer under his tongue. Lisa took his pulse; it was slightly raised. She recorded his respiration; it was quicker than normal.

Both these rises could be explained by anxiety at visiting the doctor, but she did not think so. She removed the thermometer; his temperature was minimally raised.

Lisa returned to her seat behind the desk and looked at him thoughtfully. 'Do you sweat a lot?' she asked.

'Only at night,' he said in a reluctant tone.

'Do you cough anything up?'

'Yes,' he answered roughly. Her persistence was annoying him.

Lisa wrote his replies in the notes, then glanced back to check his age. 'Did you have a Mantoux test at school?'

'What's that?' was his grumpy reply.

'A little injection under the skin of your arm.'

'No. I skipped school a lot.'

'Are you quite sure?'

'Look, Doc. There's one thing I am quite sure of and

it's that I hate the needle and would have remembered that.' His accent thickened with his aggravation.

Lisa ignored his irritation. 'I'd like Dr McKinnon to look at you,' she said.

Patrick seemed to brighten at that. 'I was supposed to see Jamie anyway.'

Lisa smiled. 'Well, you'll see him now.'

She did not want to leave the room in case Patrick left before she returned, so she dialled James's number.

'It's Dr Lisa,' she said when he answered. They always addressed each other professionally when seeing a patient.

'Well?' James sounded impatient.

'I wonder if you have a minute to spare? I have a patient I'd like you to see. He says he usually sees you anyway.'

'Can't you manage?' His tone was even more impatient.

Lisa could not very well tell him what she suspected over the phone and she could not leave Patrick, so she said, 'Not this time.'

There was a pause. Then he said, irascibly, 'Oh, very well.'

Five minutes later there was a knock on the door followed by James.

'Ah, Patrick,' he said, wondering if Patrick had been abusive, which happened sometimes, and thinking how he must tell Moira not to give the Irishman to Lisa again.

Then he took a closer look, noting Patrick's lethargy and knew that his supposition had been wrong this time.

'Well, Doctor?' James raised his eyebrow at Lisa.

She handed him the opened notes and pointed to her provisional diagnosis of pulmonary tuberculosis.

James's eyes widened. Then he frowned. 'What do you base this on?'

Lisa tapped the symptoms she had recorded with her pen.

'Hmm.' James's frown deepened. 'These could be explained away. Patrick's habit. . .' he did not want to use the word alcoholism '. . .could account for the loss of weight and appetite, also the general malaise.' He shrugged. 'And even the slight rise in temperature.'

'The sputum and the sounds in his chest?' Lisa was annoyed. Was he being deliberately obstructive because of her coolness to him this morning? Then she knew that was not the reason. James would not behave like that where a patient was concerned.

'That could be due to a chest infection,' James persisted.

'He didn't have a Mantoux or a BCG,' Lisa said, keeping her anger at bay with difficulty. 'And he has heavy night sweats.' She defended her diagnosis with spirit.

There was amusement in James's eyes as he said, 'Just testing your diagnostic skills,' and she could have killed him.

Then his face became thoughtful. 'We'll admit him and send for the radiographer.' The hospital did not have a resident one.

Lisa was pleased. He had accepted her finding.

'An X-ray will either confirm your suspicions or show Patrick had a chest infection.' He saw her pleased expression fade. 'We'll isolate him just in case, though.' And he smiled.

Lisa's face brightened.

Patrick twisted round in his chair. The doctors had been conferring in low voices behind him. 'What's all the whispering about?' he said in an agitated voice.

James came forward and perched on the edge of the desk.

'Dr Lisa tells me you've not been too well.' James's eyes examined the exhausted man in front of him, noting the tongue running over the dry lips and the tremor of Patrick's hands, symptoms of his alcoholism.

'I'm all right.' Patrick started to rise. 'If you're not going to give me the injection, I'll go. I only came this time because you said you'd track me down if I didn't.'

James grinned and, putting a hand on Patrick's shoulder, gently pushed him back on the chair. 'I want you to come into hospital so that we can X-ray your chest and do some other tests as well. See if we can get your cough better.'

Alarm widened Patrick's eyes. He rose from his chair and said, 'I'm not coming into hospital.'

'We think you might have tuberculosis,' James told him bluntly, to shock him in to agreeing to be admitted.

'You mean TB.' Patrick's pale face grew paler. 'I thought it only happened in Third World countries.'

'We still get the occasional case here,' James said.

'We-ell.' Patrick looked resigned. 'But only for a day or two,' he said quickly.

'Good.' James left the desk. 'We'll admit you now.'

'Now?' Patrick was shocked.

'Yes — now.' James's voice was firm. 'I'll take you to the ward myself.'

Lisa had remained behind Patrick. She felt he might respond better to James if she stayed in the background.

James handed her the notes as he passed her. 'See you later,' he said in a quiet voice, a question in his eyes.

'I'll look forward to it,' she replied drily.

She was just seeing her next patient, a Mrs Simpson

who had troublesome varicose veins, out of the surgery, when James returned.

'I just hope we're going to be able to keep Patrick in. I've written him up for medicinal brandy and hope that will hold him.' He saw her about to protest and said, 'Before you say anything, we've tried to stop him drinking, but to no avail. My father knows him quite well and has spent many hours trying to persuade Patrick to have treatment. The only thing he will allow us to do for him is to give him parentrovite, and that infrequently.'

James sighed. 'He hasn't a reason for drinking. No special tragedy in his life. He didn't marry,' he explained. 'He worked abroad as an engineer a lot. I think that's where his drinking really took a hold. We'll have to transfer him to the mainland if what you suspect turns out to be correct.' He took a deep breath. 'Patrick won't like that. He's a Bruig man.'

'Oh, I thought he came from Ireland,' Lisa said in surprise as she took her seat behind the desk.

'Because of his accent?' James grinned. 'His parents came over here when he was a baby and he's never lost their brogue. Like the Scots,' he said proudly. 'We always keep our accent even when we emigrate.'

'Couldn't we keep him here if he has TB?'

'It depends if his sputum is active.' He gave a shrug. 'We don't really have the facilities or the staff.' Then his face brightened. 'But when we have a bigger hospital. . .' He smiled. 'By the way, when are the plans to go forward?' His tone was even, his eyes bland. Nothing about him showed that anything more than a discussion had taken place last night. She must have been right. Their lovemaking had been just an interlude with him.

Lisa was in control of her emotions now, but her heart ached for what might have been, but never could be. Would she ever be able to give herself completely or would this fear of rejection haunt her forever?

'I thought it would be a good idea if my lawyer came to the island,' Lisa said. She did not want to go to London with James for she was afraid of what might happen. Lisa knew she would be unable to resist him if he touched her.

'Good idea.' James's tone was still bland. 'We would have had to employ a locum if we had both left the island.'

'I'll phone the lawyer at the end of surgery,' she promised.

'Good. Will I see you at coffee time?'

'No.' Lisa gestured to the pile of case-notes. 'I'm too busy.'

He had the door open when he turned back and said, 'Don't work too hard.'

She glanced up to see if he was being sarcastic, but all she saw was concern in his eyes and it was almost her undoing. She longed to rush into his arms, but dropped her eyes and reached for the top folder.

'I won't,' she said, glancing at the name. 'Could you ask Mrs Armstrong to come in, please, if you're heading to Reception?' She felt she had to say something to make him go.

'You certainly have more than your share of the female patients,' he said with a smile. 'What's your secret?'

She had to look at him then and that smile on his face was almost more than she could bear. It almost melted her resolve.

'They don't feel threatened, I suppose,' she said in what she hoped was a light tone. She opened the case-note in front of her and began to study it.

James came right up to the desk and looked down at her bent head. Her hair was coiled in a chignon and he had an insane desire to loosen it as he had yesterday.

He almost reached out, but the stiffness with which she held herself prevented him.

'And do you?' he asked quietly.

Lisa had to look up at him, look into his intent eyes. 'Do I what?' she said sharply, her expression as cold as she could make it.

James smiled slightly. 'Feel threatened?' His voice was soft.

So that's what he's thinking, Lisa thought, and said, 'I would have thought last night would have proved that I'm not afraid of men.'

James's eyes narrowed. 'I wasn't meaning it in that way. It was your. . .' He paused to find a way to explain what he meant, then said, 'Your innermost self.'

He was too intuitive. How could she answer that without giving herself away? Eventually she said 'Surely we're all afraid of that, even redoubtable Scotsmen.' Her tone was cool.

'Not if there's trust in the relationship,' he said softly, seductively. 'You mustn't let the lack of love in your childhood colour your adult relationships.'

Lisa wished she had not told him about her parents' divorce. 'Don't you think you're being a bit presumptuous?' she said, her voice cool.

James grinned. '"Faint heart never won fair lady",' he mis-quoted.

'And is that what you're about?' She touched her blonde hair. 'Out to win this fair lady?'

James was startled. She had neatly turned his analysis of her back upon himself. It was a put-up or shut-up challenge.

'Perhaps,' he said with a touch of caution.

Lisa laughed. 'You are funny.' The tension she had been feeling left her. 'You're so busy trying to decide why I haven't fallen into your arms this morning.' Her eyes were amused and just a little cynical. 'Why?'

James put his hands on the desk, those capable surgeon's hands, and leaned forward until his face was so close to hers that she could see where he had missed a bit shaving. She had to clasp her hands tightly in her lap to stop them reaching up to pull his head down to kiss him.

Her mockery goaded him into saying, 'Because I thought there was something more between us than just a strong physical attraction.'

'More?' The word whispered from her lips.

'Yes, more, damn you.' James reached forward and pulled the pins from her hair, unable to restrain himself any longer.

Taking her face in his hands, he searched her eyes and saw there the love she could no longer hide. 'Lisa,' he whispered. 'I love you, don't you know that?'

His hands fell from her face. He was round the desk and she was in his arms, his lips upon hers, her arms around him, and the ache, which had lived in her heart since childhood, was cured.

All thoughts that he was using her, that he wanted to control her money to use for the hospital, were swept away by his kisses.

When they broke apart, the coldness had left her expression. Her mouth, which was inclined to be tight, had softened. The wariness had gone from her eyes. Even her body in his arms felt different in a subtle way.

'Are you free this evening?' he asked, his voice rough with emotion. Then his eyes became thoughtful. 'What do you spend your evenings doing, by the way?'

Lisa laughed. 'I study my medical books. How do you think I diagnosed Patrick?'

James gave her a wry look. 'It's not confirmed yet.'

She patted his chest. 'It will be.'

He put his arms round her and she put hers around

his waist. 'I think you deserve a night away from your books.'

'I had one last night if you remember.' Her eyes were laughing.

'That was business.' He grinned.

'Monkey business!' She laughed.

'I'll pick you up at seven,' he said, a smile on his face as they walked, arms around each other, to the door.

'Is that a promise?' She raised her face to his.

'Indeed it is,' he whispered before he kissed her.

As the kiss threatened to overwhelm them, she pushed him away. 'Duty calls,' she said with a tremor in her voice.

James gave a big sigh. 'Ah, yes. So it does.'

That evening James arrived exactly at seven. He had not told her where he was taking her, so Lisa had just put on a simple blue linen dress. It was collarless with short sleeves and a straight skirt. The matching jacket was just heavy enough for the cool evening breezes. Her shoes and handbag were of the same colour.

Lisa had expected him to arrive in the Range Rover, so was surprised, as she stepped from the house to see a red sports car in the drive. It was an old model, but in pristine condition. Rory was sitting in the bucket seat at the back. He barked when he saw her. They had become firm friends and she took him with her on her visiting round.

As James seated her in the passenger seat Rory licked the right side of her face. 'I think he likes the taste of your make-up,' James said with a smile. 'I like it, too.'

Lisa laughed. 'Down, boy,' she said to Rory, but she was looking at James, who laughed.

It was a fine evening on the last day of May. The sky was blue, but a cool breeze blew in from the sea as

James took the coast road. The wind lifted her hair, which she had left loose.

'Would you like the top up?' James asked.

'No, thanks. I love to feel the wind in my hair.' She smiled. 'I suppose you get as much use out of this car as I do with mine?'

'Yes.' James kept his eyes on the road. 'I keep it to remind me. It's a symbol of the past.'

'Do you ever regret coming back to the island? With your surgical skill you could have been a senior consultant by now.'

'Probably, but I got fed up with all that bureaucracy.' He shrugged. 'I thought of going abroad and came back to the island to think.' He glanced about him. 'Things always seem so much clearer here.' He was silent while he slowed the car to take a bend. 'This post was about to fall vacant and I suddenly decided to apply for it. I had already trained as a GP before deciding to become a surgeon, so I was qualified.' He gave her a quick glance. 'I've never regretted it.'

The road took another turn and the bay came into sight. It was bigger than the bay where the Andersons lived; there were more houses, a small hotel and some shops. It even had a small supermarket. Lisa had been here before to visit a patient. There were only the usual cafés, so she presumed they must be dining at the hotel until James passed it and took the road leading up the hill on the other side of the town.

A few houses were scattered haphazardly as if the builder had kept changing his mind as to where to place them.

James took a turning to the left and finally stopped outside a charming house at the end of the road. It was built so that the half-circle bay windows overlooked the sea. It had stout stone walls, a pointed roof, grey slates and white paintwork. It wasn't large and yet it gave the appearance of being so.

Lisa loved it immediately. The garden in the front was small and laid out in grass with a path dividing it. The gate, which led on to the path, creaked as James opened it.

'I always forget to oil it,' he said with a grin.

There was a porch with a pointed roof, protecting the front door. Red geraniums lined the shelves on either side. The floor was stone.

James took her into the house. Lisa had expected the hall to be dark, but it wasn't. A window on the landing brightened it and the light-coloured wallpaper ensured that there were no dark corners.

He opened the door into the lounge for her to precede him. It was big and here again the walls were light, almost white. Paintings of the sea should have made the room seem cold, but the soft brown leather armchairs, combined with a multi-patterned coloured carpet, gave it warmth.

There was a bookcase containing well-used books; occasional chairs with velvet seats. No coffee-table, but small tables stood beside the chairs, like waiters expecting an order. Heavy dark blue curtains hung either side of the window. There were family photographs on the mantelpiece. Medical journals, fishing magazines and newspapers were strewn on the floor beside the armchairs.

Lisa crossed to the window-seat and sat down. The view had drawn her. It was stupendous, stretching across the bay to the mountains beyond.

'I'm glad you like the house,' James said. He had no need to ask, it was there in her eyes.

'I love it,' she said simply.

'But you haven't seen the rest.'

'I don't need to,' Lisa said softly. And he knew what she meant. Some houses were like that.

'Would you like a drink before dinner?' he asked.

'No,' she said, smiling, her face alight with happiness.

James came to her and, taking her hand, drew her to her feet and into his arms. He kissed her gently on the lips.

Somehow this seemed right. This was not a house, it was a home. A warm, loving home. A place where those who made love were committed to each other in more than just love. Committed not just physically, but spiritually.

Lisa loved James, but she could not allow herself to listen to her heart even though it cried out for her to do just that. She was afraid to marry him. Afraid to lose what they had.

She would have liked to live with him, but that was impossible on Bruig where the old values were too strong, and Lisa felt that James, in spite of his sophistication, would not enter into a long-standing relationship without marriage.

The blueness of the sky was swept away by dark clouds, just as the troubled expression in Lisa's eyes swept away the happiness James had seen there.

His face became serious. 'Why so worried, sweetheart?'

The endearment brought tears to her eyes. She could not tell him that she wasn't sure that she wanted to marry him when he had not asked her, so she said, giving him a quick kiss, 'I'm worried that you're not going to feed me,' in a teasing tone.

James laughed. He knew that wasn't what was bothering her, but he didn't persist. Taking her hand, he said, 'Come on.'

The appetising smell met Lisa as soon as she entered the kitchen. 'Hannah, our housekeeper, has left everything ready. I hope you like Scotch broth, he said, taking a large covered pot from the oven and filling two bowls without waiting for her reply.

'Yes,' Lisa said. Janet had introduced her to the thick nourishing soup.

He carried the bowls on a tray into the dining-room. A telescope stood in the window. Pictures of sailing ships hung on the walls. The table and chairs were mahogany.

James put the bowls on the places already set, then pulled out a chair for her.

'Thank you. I must say the service is excellent,' she joked.'

'I'm glad you're pleased, madam.' He grinned. 'Of course, I'll expect a tip.'

Lisa took a mouthful of the broth and nearly burnt her tongue. A sip of water from a glass he hastily filled helped to cool her mouth.

'A tip?' She frowned. 'I don't know if I can afford that.' She smiled, but her eyes were serious.

James reached forward and took her hand. 'You can afford this one, sweetheart. I want you to marry me right away,' he said, his eyes smiling.

It was his saying 'right away' that suddenly alarmed Lisa, and the thought that he might only love her money slithered back into her mind. She took a sip of the now cooled soup to moisten her dry mouth.

James frowned. He had expected an immediate acceptance; he had not thought that she would need to think about it. He knew she loved him and he loved her. His soup was left untasted.

Lisa put down her spoon and faced him. 'I don't know that I want to get married yet,' she said quietly.

'What do you mean?' His frown deepened. 'When people are in love they usually get married.'

Lisa could hear the anger in his voice, but said, 'Not

necessarily,' more sharply than she meant to. She could not understand why he was so angry. 'In this day and age couples can be in love without surrendering their independence. . .' It wasn't really what she meant.

'Is that how you look upon marriage — that you're losing your independence?' He was really angry now, but Lisa was determined not to let him upset her.

She shrugged and said, 'In a way — yes.'

It made matters worse. James leaned back in his chair. 'You are afraid of me,' he said more quietly.

He was right about her fear, but it was not of him physically. Lisa threw down her serviette.

'Oh, don't be silly.' She was becoming exasperated. 'Of course I'm not. I don't know what you're making such a fuss about. What difference does a ring make if two people are sincere in their relationship?'

There was truth in what she said. 'If you're thinking about our living together,' he said, 'it won't work on Bruig and you know why.' His face was tight. 'We would lose the respect of our patients.'

The patients — the hospital, that's all he thinks about, moaned Lisa to herself.

'Can't we go on as we are?' she said a little plaintively. 'After all, we need to get to know each other.'

It sounded so reasonable and she looked so anxious that James relented. He reached for her hand. 'Yes, of course.' He smiled. 'I'm sorry I flew off the handle. I was disappointed.' He rose. 'I'll bring the main course. You sit there.' He collected the plates.

The rest of the meal passed amicably, and yet Lisa sensed an underlying aggravation in James. The frown lines between his eyes had not lifted completely.

They were eating a delicious raspberry mousse when he said, 'I thought Janet was looking better today when I popped in for a moment.'

'Yes, she is. The rest has helped, but I had a job to get her to stay put.'

James's grin was more natural as he said, 'She worries. It'll help her if her niece accepts the sister's post.'

'But what about references?' Lisa did not want to bring Karen into this lovely house even in speech, but this was an opportunity for her to try and persuade James not to accept her one-time friend.

'Janet's recommendation is enough for me, but of course we'll ask for references.'

'But what about Sarah?'

'Our relief sister?'

'Yes.'

'Well, as you know, she's only part-time, and with small children I doubt if she would be willing to increase her hours.'

'But don't you think she should be given the chance?' Lisa insisted.

'She hasn't the experience.' It was spoken with a finality that would brook no reply. James was wearing his consultant's hat. 'And we're going to need an experienced theatre sister when your hospital opens.'

'It's not my hospital,' Lisa said sharply. 'It's the island's hospital.'

'And what's it to be called?' Her tone aggravated him into adding, 'The Charles Halliman Memorial Hospital?' He could not keep the sarcasm out of his voice.

'Don't you think you're being a bit childish to allow a dead man to affect you so?' Lisa was astonished and spoke up spiritedly.

He gave her sheepish look. 'You're right. I'm sorry, but you Hallimans have a way of aggravating people.'

'That's how we get where we are. We're ruthless.' And she smiled.

CHAPTER NINE

THE lawyers came to the island during the first week in June. A trust fund was set up and money made available. In the second week, James and Lisa discussed the renovations of Halliman House with Ben Anderson's brother, Ian, who was holidaying on the island. His firm of architects was well-known and had a sound reputation.

The evenings were the most suitable time for the doctors. But Lisa discovered she was not too pleased at the way James appeared to be organising everything.

'I think we should convert these rooms. . .' James pointed to four of the rooms upstairs detailed on the plans 'into two theatres.' His finger moved over. 'We could put a lift in here. What do you think, Ian?' It was as if Lisa were not there.

Ian thought for a moment and then said, 'Yes, I think that would be possible. Are you proposing to have the male and female surgical wards upstairs as well?' He glanced at James.

'Yes.'

Lisa, who was fuming inwardly, was just about to say, I think that would be a good idea as well, when James turned to her and said, 'What do you think, Doctor?' with a twinkle in his eye. He had guessed she was about to explode.

It wasn't his deferring to her that swept her annoyance away, it was his heart-melting smile. It gripped her every time.

'Yes,' she agreed, her voice just above a whisper.

'That's my girl,' he said softly.

Ian glanced from one to the other. His sister-in-law, Shirley, had hinted that there was more than a professional relationship between the two doctors, but Ian had thought it was just Shirley's romantic soul talking. Now he suspected that she was right. Pity, because Lisa was a very attractive woman and with all that money as well. Ian was a little surprised, though, that James should have been smitten. He knew, from his brother, how James had hated Charles Halliman.

Ian glanced down at the plans with a frown. Then he said, his face clearing, 'I know why this house seems so familiar. I remember now. The man who owned the island before your father had the same idea.' He smiled. 'My father was asked to draw up plans for the conversion of the house into a hospital then. I'll go over to the mainland tomorrow and bring them back.'

James was curious. 'Why didn't he go ahead with it?'

Ian pulled a face. 'It was too expensive.' He looked at Lisa. 'And it will be even more expensive now.'

Lisa shrugged. 'I'm sure we'll manage.'

The three of them were having after-dinner coffee at Halliman House. It was Friday evening.

'It would be a good idea if we could build some sheltered housing in the grounds.' She pushed the after-dinner mints across to the two men and looked at James. 'I visited Sheena today and she really is becoming frail. Not only that, her sister's arthritis is making it difficult for her to look after Sheena properly.' She took a sip of coffee. 'There's that stretch of land not far from the house overlooking the sea that might suit.'

'Was it a block or separate houses you were thinking of?' Ian asked. James had made no comment.

'Small houses in a croft-like style so that the elderly, especially those who have lived in crofts all their lives, would feel at home.' Lisa tucked her loose hair behind her ears. 'It would be an added advantage, the hospital

being in the same grounds.' She glanced at James.
There was a small frown on his face. Had she made it
too obvious that it was her money that was making all
this possible? Was his pride hurting? She hoped not.

'What do you think, Doctor?'

The frown left his face. That he could not command
the amount of money at Lisa's disposal was unfortunate, but her suggestion was excellent, so he grinned at
her teasing tone and said, 'I think it's a great idea, but
the added cost. . . It must not mean that the hospital
will be skimped.' His face was serious.

'We'll have to see,' she said, a bit annoyed that he
would shelve her plan if it threatened the hospital.

They discussed further details, then Ian looked at his
watch. 'Time I was going,' he said, looking at Lisa.
'Thanks for a delicious meal.' He grinned. 'And for the
charming company.'

'I take it that includes me?' James said with a smile.

'Definitely not,' said Ian, the grin still on his face. 'I
was referring to the lady.' He bowed.

Lisa laughed. Ian really was a charmer, but in a nice
way. He must be a year or two older than James, about
thirty-seven, she supposed, and good company. He had
made her laugh on quite a few occasions over the last
few days; their sense of humour was the same, but
James had not been pleased at the rapport between
them.

She had teased him about it and said, 'You don't
have to worry, darling, he's only after my money,' and
she had laughed.

James had reddened at the time and she had thought
it rather sweet.

This evening, Lisa walked between the two men to
the front door. On the step, Ian turned to them both.

'Oh, I nearly forgot. Shirley and Ben wondered if

you would both like to go sailing this weekend? Tomorrow if the weather's fine.'

Lisa's face brightened. 'I'm available, but poor James is on duty.'

James sighed. 'Alas, yes.'

Ian grinned. 'Your loss is my gain,' he said, and, taking Lisa's hand, raised it to his lips.

She laughed. James smiled, but his smile was a bit tight.

Ian had taken a couple of steps when he turned back and said, 'Where are you going to live, Lisa, when work starts on the house?'

She looked blank. 'I hadn't thought about it,' and gave a light laugh.

'You can have my flat at the hospital,' said James. 'I'll live at home.'

Lisa did not relish living in such stark accommodation, but it would do until she decided where she would live.

'Thanks,' she said and smiled at James. 'It'll do as a stopgap.'

'A stopgap?' He looked hopeful and grinned.

Lisa laughed. Ian looked puzzled. 'Just a joke,' she said.

'Would you like me to collect you tomorrow?' Ian offered.

'No, thanks. I'll meet you at the yacht club. What time?'

'About ten.'

'Right.'

James put his arm round Lisa's waist as they waved goodbye. 'Did you have to sound so eager?' he asked, a little disgruntled.

Lisa turned in his arms and touched his face. 'I love it when you're jealous.'

James grinned. 'I just don't trust you with Ian. He's too charming.'

'Now then, you're the one whose always talking about trust,' she said mischievously. 'And here you are. . .' His kiss stopped her, and when he let her go she said softly, 'It's you I love.'

'But not enough.' He frowned.

Lisa pulled out of his arms. 'Don't pressure me, James,' she said, the smile leaving her face.

'I'd better go.' There was a touch of impatience in his voice. 'Have a nice weekend.'

'I'll see you, though, won't I.' She hoped she did not sound plaintive.

'Janet's niece is arriving tomorrow. I told Janet I'd meet the ferry.' Seeing what appeared to James to be a look of surprise, but was actually shock, he said, 'I forgot to tell you. It was your mentioning seeing me at the weekend that reminded me.'

He gave her a quick kiss and was gone.

Lisa was distressed that his kiss had been so offhand. She did not wait to see his car go, but turned back into the house. She had forgotten all about Karen. Her love for James had swept all other thoughts aside, but now her memories of the dark-haired girl seemed to join with the discordance left by Lisa's parents, so that the atmosphere in the house became cold, almost threatening and Lisa shivered.

She hurried through the hall and up to her bedroom, but it was no different there. She did not bother to shower, but quickly undressed and jumped into bed. The sheets were cold and seemed to take ages to warm.

Her dreams were like nightmares with her parents' and Karen's faces distorted, like those seen through a door's peep-hole.

The alarm clock was set for nine, but she was awake well before then, and was showered and dressed in jeans, T-shirt and jumper, her hair in a long plait, when it went off.

She was glad she was going sailing. It would occupy her mind, stop her thinking of Karen. At least I won't see her until Monday, she thought. But in this she was mistaken.

When Lisa arrived at the harbour she found only Ian waiting for her.

'A rush order was faxed in this morning,' he explained, 'so Shirley and Ben can't come, but they want us to have dinner with them this evening.' He had a broad grin on his face.

'Are you sure you didn't arrange for the order yourself?' Lisa asked with a wry look. She was fully aware that Ian was attracted to her.

He laughed. 'No, but if I had thought of it. . .'

Lisa joined in his laughter.

'We can manage the boat between us,' he said. 'Shirley told me you're an excellent sailor.'

It was an ideal day — blue skies, warm sun and just the right amount of wind. They saw the ferry crossing while they were out, and the thought of who it was carrying clouded Lisa's enjoyment.

'I've booked a table at the yacht club for one-thirty,' Ian said as he came and sat beside her at the tiller, his arm carelessly flung across her shoulders. His eyes were mischievous.

Lisa gave him a 'now then' look and he removed it. His eyes were twinkling as he said, 'I was only protecting you. It wouldn't do for you to fall overboard.'

She laughed. 'An experienced sailor like myself avoids those dangers. It's the two-legged variety I have to watch out for.'

They both laughed. Lisa was far more relaxed with Ian than she was with James. Ian was fun to be with and she glanced at him affectionately.

Seeing this, Ian put his arm around her shoulders again. She lifted it off and said, 'Now, now.'

'Private property?' His smile was a trifle wistful.

'You could say that,' she told him gently,

'Ah — well.' Ian sighed.

They arrived back at one o'clock. 'I'll jump out,' he said as they neared the quay. 'You throw the rope.'

Ian leapt, but had misjudged the distance and went into the water. Lisa's laugh turned to horror when she saw the water turning red as he surfaced. His face was white with shock.

'Damn piece of jagged iron down there,' he said. 'Caught my leg on it.'

Lisa did not know where she found the strength to haul Ian into the boat, but she did. He was as tall as James, but of a heavier build. His face was almost grey with blood loss.

The wound was deep and as Lisa rushed to the small cabin to catch up a towel and two rugs she decided that he had probably cut the femoral artery. On her return she quickly whipped off his belt and pulled off his trousers and applied the belt round his thigh above the six-inch wound.

'Taking advantage of me?' Ian said, his smile turning to a grimace of pain.

Lisa elevated his leg by propping his ankle on the tiller seat and wound the towel round the wound. 'Shh,' she said gently.

He was starting to shiver as she wrapped him in the rugs. 'Oooh, you are going to take advantage of my helpless condition,' he said with a weak grin as he saw her strip off her jumper and fold it.

'Not this time,' she said, placing it under his head as a pillow.

'I like that perfume.' He sniffed appreciatively, but his voice was becoming fainter and Lisa was very worried. She checked the towel; the blood was soaking through it.

'I'm just going to get some help to lift you,' Lisa told him.

'I'll get up.' He tried to raise himself, but fell back with a groan.

'Just lie still,' Lisa said in a firm voice.

'OK, Doc.' His smile did not quite make it.

It was lunchtime at the club so Lisa was back with two large men within moments. Ian was barely conscious. They lifted him easily between them, leaving behind a red stain on the deck.

Lisa's car was impractical so one of the men drove Ian and herself to the hospital in his hatchback. The other man had phoned the hospital, so James met them at the entrance. Lisa was more than glad to see him.

She did not need to say anything. One look was enough for James. Ian was on the trolley and on the way to Theatre before the driver was out of the gate.

'Well?' James smiled down at Ian as they lifted him on to the operating table, 'What did she do? Push you in?'

'No.' Ian's smile was strained. 'Fished me out.'

'We'll have to sew this up, and quickly. Do you consent to an operation?'

'You twisted my arm.' Ian tried to joke, but his face was pinched with pain.

A transfusion of plasma was erected within seconds. Lisa had left the theatre staff to help James transfer Ian to the table. She had put on her mask and gown and had her back to them as she checked the anaesthetic machine, then her concentration was directed at anaesthetising her patient.

It wasn't until James returned with the theatre nurses after scrubbing and robing in green that she became aware that one of the nurses was to assist him.

'Ready?' James asked Lisa, who nodded.

She looked more closely at the nurse handing the instruments to James and realised it was Janet. She would have something to say to the matron when the emergency was over. Janet should not be working.

There was something familiar about the other nurse who was assisting, but it wasn't until he said, 'Mop that bit, Karen, please,' that Lisa knew who the figure was — Karen Carmichael.

'Oh,' said James suddenly. 'In all the rush we forgot to introduce you to Janet's niece.' He glanced from Lisa to Karen. 'Karen Carmichael — Lisa Halliman.'

Now was the time to tell James that she knew Karen, but she didn't; she just nodded and applied herself to her job.

Karen couldn't have said anything either, and Lisa wondered why. Her hand trembled as she checked the oxygen flow.

'Is he all right?' James asked without looking at her, his concentration reserved for the patient.

'Yes,' Lisa said.

She looked up and her eyes met Karen's. Hate stared back at her. James did not see the interchange; he was busy repairing Ian's muscle.

A short time later, he tied the last stitch.

'Cut,' he said, his eyes smiling at Karen. She returned the smile and cut the threads.

'Very competently assisted,' James complimented Karen. 'Lucky you were here.' He smiled across at Janet. 'We'll finish off. You go and rest.' Karen was dressing the wound.

'Thanks.' Janet pulled down her mask.

'I'll come and see you as soon as I've finished,' Lisa said, concerned at how tired Janet looked. 'You shouldn't be here.'

'Sarah has a cold,' Janet explained quietly.

Lisa felt stupid, especially as James and Karen were both looking at her—James's expression showed surprise and Karen's face was bland, except for her eyes, which showed pleasure at Lisa's discomfort.

This annoyed her. Instead of returning Karen's look with a bland expression, she glared at the dark-haired woman, and it was this glare that James saw. He immediately thought she was jealous.

'I'll be in the flat,' Janet said and blushed. She had thought Lisa's expression was directed at herself.

Lisa, realising this, gave her a smile. 'Good.'

She concentrated on her care of Ian, trying to close her ears as James praised Karen's bandaging.

'You must have had plenty of practice,' he said.

'I did quite a bit of casualty work when I was in Australia.' Karen had pulled down her mask and gave James a brilliant smile.

'You must tell me all about your experiences there,' he said, returning her smile.

I bet her experiences would get an X rating, thought Lisa uncharitably.

'I hope you're going to put a crêpe bandage on top of that cling bandage,' she said grimly.

'Of course she is.' James was positively glowing and Lisa could have killed him, especially as Karen responded with a seductive smile.

Lisa bent her head to Ian, carefully monitoring his rise to consciousness.

'You'll take him back to the ward, won't you, Lisa, while I go and change?' James said in an offhand way.

She had been going to accompany her patient anyway and James should have known that. There was no need for him to suggest it.

'Yes,' she said in a tight voice and glared at him this time, but he had turned away, so his back received her look of displeasure.

Karen also had turned, but she glanced back at Lisa, a smug look in her eyes.

As Lisa took Ian to the ward she wondered if James was inviting Karen to share his shower, knowing that Karen would have accepted with alacrity.

He had arranged for their only side-ward to be prepared for Ian. Lisa stayed with him until he was fully round from the anaesthetic, but all the time she watched over him her mind was with Karen and James. What was Karen telling him?

Lisa was so preoccupied that she did not see Ian open his eyes. It was his slurred, 'Hi, Doc,' that alerted her.

She smiled down at him. 'How do you feel?'

'Woozy.' He frowned.

'You'll be fine soon,' she assured him. 'Don't move your arm, you've still got the drip in. We're giving you some blood.'

There was a bed-cradle over his leg. She lifted the bedclothes and looked at the bandage. There was no sign of blood oozing through it.

His eyelids were becoming heavy. 'Thanks for saving my life,' he said, his words running into each other.

Lisa smoothed back the hair from his forehead. 'Any time,' she said.

She went into the ward and had a word with the nurse. Then she phoned Shirley and Ben from her surgery to let them know where Ian was.

'But it's not serious, is it?' Ben asked, sounding anxious.

'No. He's lost a lot of blood, but we're replacing it. He should be as good as new in a week's time. We'll ask the physiotherapist to come and see him.'

'Thanks for all you've done,' Ben said.

'James did the operation.'

'Thank him for us, will you? We'll see him when we come in.'

'I'll do that.' Lisa rang off.

She changed out of her blood-stained jeans into a pair of pale blue trousers that she had collected from the cleaners yesterday. Lisa had been annoyed to discover, when she had arrived home, that she had left them at the surgery, but she was glad of it now.

Opening the surgery door, she heard James laugh and almost bumped into him as she stepped into the corridor. Karen was on his arm.

'How's Ian?' he said in a casual way. It seemed to Lisa that he was fully occupied with the theatre sister, who was looking very smart in an expensive green linen dress which had definitely not been bought in a chain store. The colour drew attention to the dark girl's sparkling green eyes. A honey-coloured tan added to Karen's attractiveness. James was wearing grey trousers with a grey designer shirt. He looked magnificent and Lisa could see that Karen thought so too.

'He's fine.'

'I was just taking Karen for a spot of lunch at the Bruig Arms. Care to come?'

His invitation sounded as if it was an afterthought and Lisa was disturbed.

'I have to see how Janet is.'

'I've already seen her. She's fine.'

'Then I'll come.'

Lisa knew how clever Karen was at manipulating men and she wasn't going to let the dark girl steal James.

Karen's face stiffened, but she said nothing.

James told the receptionist where they would be and said, 'I'll pop in after lunch to see how everything is.'

He tucked an arm of each woman into his on either side of him. 'It's not often that I have two beautiful women to escort,' he said, giving them both a smile.

Lisa gave him a sickly grin in return and could

imagine the smile Karen was giving him. One of her best 'I think you're wonderful' smiles.

His sports car was outside. Didn't meet her in the Range Rover, then, was Lisa's jaundiced thought.

'You don't mind sitting in the bucket seat, do you, Lisa?' Not darling, just Lisa, she noted.

Lisa did, but she smiled sweetly and said, 'Of course not, James.'

She saw an amused twinkle enter his eyes and this aggravated her further so that she fumed all the way to the hotel.

The restaurant at the Bruig Arms was adequate, but not special. Lisa could not even be glad about that, because it was the only decent restaurant on the island apart from cafés, but the food was good.

As they took the menu from the waiter, James said, 'You must try our haggis; I'm sure it must be on the menu.'

'Oh, I love haggis,' gushed Karen.

She would, thought Lisa, who was not too fond of it herself and chose the fish.

'Chicken.' James grinned at her.

Lisa deliberately misunderstood him and said, 'No, fish, please,' with a straight face.

James smiled and gave their orders.

'You know, Lisa, it isn't only a hospital that we need on the island. We could do more to improve the tourist trade.' He was becoming enthusiastic. 'Now that you own the island ——'

'Own the island?' Karen interrupted him, her eyes round, her mouth almost agape.

James turned to her. 'Yes,' he said. 'Lisa's father was Charles Halliman the entrepreneur. He left Bruig to Lisa in his will.'

'Really?' Karen looked at Lisa. 'But I thought he hated you, Lisa.'

Now Lisa understood why Karen had not mentioned knowing her. Karen knew Lisa had not told James so she had waited for an opportunity to present itself to divulge the information, so as to discredit Lisa.

James's jaw dropped. His surprise was complete.

'You know each other?' He looked at Lisa. Why hadn't she told him?

'Oh, yes. Didn't Lisa tell you? Karen brushed a strand of hair from her forehead. 'We went to school together and then worked in the same London hospital. If it weren't for me, Lisa would have had to face a medical board. She left a swab in a patient.' She was all innocence. 'If I hadn't been meticulous in my swab count. . .' She shrugged.

Lisa was so stunned that she missed the opportunity to defend herself and could only stare in horror.

James, seeing what appeared to him to be Lisa's guilt, said, 'That's very serious.' His face was grim.

Karen took advantage of Lisa's speechlessness and said, 'Yes, but all was well,' in a tone implying that it wouldn't have been if she had not been there.

James smiled his approval.

Lisa struggled to find a way out of the trap Karen had dropped her in. If she told the truth James would think that she was trying to implicate Karen unjustly. All surgeons knew it was the theatre sister's job to ensure the swab count was correct, and who could doubt the honesty shining in Karen's eyes?

But Lisa wasn't going to let her surgical integrity be in question, not for James, not for anyone, so she said, 'Yes.' She looked directly at Karen. 'It's a pity this meticulous count came too late.'

As soon as the words left her mouth Lisa knew she had phrased her defence badly, especially as Karen just raised a sarcastic eyebrow, which implied that Lisa was making a pathetic attempt to cover her fault.

James's grim expression did not soften as he looked at Lisa. Even though she was looking back at him she could feel Karen's gloating and knew the dark-haired girl's face would be set in sympathetic lines. Karen knew she had won, for what could Lisa say now that would not make matters worse?

'And why didn't you tell me you knew Karen?' he said, his voice sharp-edged, upset that Lisa had not answered.

She could hear the hurt behind the tense words. He was frowning as he said, 'I thought you trusted me?'

Karen looked from James to Lisa. They were talking as if she were not there. Her aunt had mentioned that the two doctors worked well together, but she had not said there was a special relationship between the two. But then Janet was not a gossip. That there was a relationship was plain to Karen. The look on both their faces was enough — the hurt behind James's eyes, the distress in Lisa's. Karen was amazed to see such emotion in Lisa's eyes. She had always thought the blonde girl was cold, but now. . .

Karen almost licked her lips in glee. She had never forgiven Lisa for the incident in the operating theatre. Now she was in a position to do something about it.

But none of this showed in her face.

When Lisa still did not speak, James's face became hard. 'I suppose you did not want Karen to accept the post because I would find out about your lapse?'

This can't be happening, Lisa told herself and her heart ached at the thought of losing James's love, but what could she do? What could she say?

The soup had arrived and she still had not spoken.

'This looks good,' Karen said as if nothing had happened.

James shook his napkin out and spread it over his knees. 'Yes,' he said shortly, then relented his brusqueness. After all, Karen was the innocent catalyst, so he said, 'I hope you enjoy it,' and smiled.

It was what Lisa thought of as her smile, the one that left her bereft of speech — the one that always made her want to throw her arms around his neck. That he should be directing it at that snake of a woman was too much.

She shot to her feet; the water slopped out of her glass as she did so. 'Well, you can enjoy it together,' she said and swept out of the dining-room and out of the hotel, her head held so erect that her neck ached.

To hell with him. To hell with Karen. Thank goodness her car was still at the quay.

CHAPTER TEN

LISA drove swiftly back to the hospital, almost hitting the gatepost as she swung into the drive. She checked Ian was all right and then drove home.

By the time she reached the house her anger had left her and she realised how foolish she had been. The way was open for Karen now and Lisa knew the dark-haired girl would take full advantage of it. She had seen how Karen had looked at James — sensually and James's eyes had lit up with more than interest.

The house was empty. Lisa was glad it was Jean's day off. In the bedroom, she stripped off her clothes and had a shower. As she turned her face up to the warm water, she wondered if anything had happened between James and Karen when Janet's niece had visited the island before. He was certainly attracted to her.

If only she could wash away her misery as easily as she could the soap from her body, thought Lisa. What were the two of them doing now? Visions of them making love rose to torment her. Were his hands touching Karen as they had touched her?

There had not been a recurrence of their passionate lovemaking since that evening in this house. James had said she should have the time she wanted and that they should control the physical side of their love. He wanted her to be sure that when she said yes to his next marriage proposal their future would be based on more than their intense physical attraction.

Lisa rubbed herself down, and dressed in beige trousers and a cotton short-sleeved jumper which had a crocheted collar. She had just dried and plaited her hair and was twisting a band to put round the end when she heard the bell.

The band dropped to the floor. Her hair loosened as she ran, her feet barely touching the stairs in her haste to reach the front door. Lisa flung it open and there he was, tall, lean, dark and serious.

She flung herelf into his arms, crying, 'I love you, I love you,' her tears wet upon his cheeks.

His arms tightened about her. His lips found hers again and again with an urgency only equalled by her own. He swept her up into his arms, but she barely noticed; her lips were still clinging to his, her arms around his neck.

Lisa was aware of the softness of the white rug — she had been unable to give it away — touching her bare skin, but only because it contrasted with the hardness of his body.

Their enforced abstinence made their lovemaking more intense. There was a wildness about it; their need was so great. Again and yet again they sought satisfaction from each other until, finally sated, they fell asleep, their arms about each other.

The cooling of their bodies woke them. Laughing, they ran naked like Adam and Eve up to her bedroom and into the shower. Putting on their clothes swept away their almost primitive coming together, but it still lingered in their eyes.

'Now will you marry me?' he whispered as they sat close together on the couch, mugs of coffee before them on the low table.

Maybe if she staked her claim her fear that Karen would take him from her would vanish, and she knew it would please James if she accepted, so she said, 'Yes.'

He took her into his arms and kissed her. The urgency had gone, but even so, their coffee became cold as their lips met and their arms tightened about each other.

The only blight on her happiness came as they stood at the front door.

'Forget the past,' James said. 'And try to get on with Karen.' He gave her a kiss. 'I wish I could stay, but I have a patient to see.'

It was as the door closed behind him that Lisa wondered if that was why he had made love to her. Smooth working relations were essential for the hospital's success.

But she pushed these thoughts aside. He was not martyring himself when he made love to her. He was genuine and she could not bring herself to believe that it was lust, not love.

She was just crossing the hall when the phone rang. It was Shirley. 'I'm phoning from the hospital. Ben and I have just visited Ian. He's fine and he still wants you to have dinner with us. Will you come?'

Lisa had been looking forward to seeing Shirley; she enjoyed the other woman's chatter as long as it wasn't about James and herself, so she said, 'That would be very nice.'

'Good. See you about eight o'clock, then.'

'Fine.'

When Lisa arrived at the Andersons', Ben opened the door. Lisa could hear voices coming from the lounge, and at first thought James must have been invited, but then she realised one of the voices was Karen's.

'We've invited a friend of yours.' Shirley rose from the couch. 'The new theatre sister, Karen Carmichael. James introduced us when we visited Ian.'

That Shirley had thought she was pleasing Lisa was obvious by the happy smile on her face, so there was nothing that Lisa could do except smile in return.

It was when Karen said, from her seat on the couch, 'It was lovely to find Lisa here. We were at school together. My aunt didn't tell me. She saved it for a surprise,' that Lisa wanted to laugh out loud. She could imagine what a surprise it had been. But she was disturbed. Karen was more dangerous than she had thought.

She knew that she would either have to treat Karen coolly or pretend to a friendship she did not feel. It was all her own fault. She should have told James about her when Janet had proposed her niece. But how could she have blurted out Karen's blunder when Janet's angina had just been diagnosed? The shock might have been too great. Karen, obviously, had not mentioned the incident in the theatre to her aunt.

Well, Lisa thought, I'll just have to do the best I can. No good moaning. Perhaps if she played Karen at her own game. . .? So she said, 'Yes. It was quite a surprise,' and the understatement brought a grin to her face. The moment passed more easily that she could have hoped.

It also brought some satisfaction, for Karen's eyes showed a moment of doubt. Good, thought Lisa. It's her turn to wonder what I'm up to.

Shirley had prepared the only dish she was good at making — lasagne — and it was delicious. The conversation during the meal was interesting. Karen told them about Australia.

'You didn't want to stay there?' Shirley's eyes were bright. 'No nice young man?'

'Nothing special.' Karen's tone implied that there had been quite a few. 'I prefer my own countrymen, especially the Scots.'

'I admire your good taste,' said Ben with a laugh.

As Shirley cut into an apple pie, she said, with a smile, 'All the attractive Scotsmen on this island have been taken.' She handed a filled plate to Lisa. 'Isn't that so, Lisa?'

Lisa poured some cream on to her pie. 'Well, James certainly has.' She smiled across at Karen. 'I've just accepted his proposal.'

Shirley dropped the knife she had been using and rushed round the table to give Lisa a hug.

'Oh, how marvellous,' she enthused. 'When's the wedding?'

'Hold on, Shirley.' Lisa laughed. 'We only became engaged today. I wouldn't have told you, but I shouldn't like Karen to get her hopes up.' The look she gave Karen said, So keep your hands off my man.

Karen gave a tinkling laugh. 'Oh, that's a pity. I had my eye on him myself.'

Lisa detected a challenge behind the jesting words, a touch of hardness in the smiling eyes. It was as if she had said, You're not married yet.

Ben refilled their glasses, except for Lisa, who was driving.

'Here's to you both,' he said, raising his glass. 'Sorry it's not champagne.'

After they had finished their meal, Shirley said, 'We'll have coffee in the lounge and I'll show you our wedding photographs.' Her eyes were bright with excitement.

The rest of the evening was spent with Shirley recounting her wedding in detail. At eleven o'clock, Lisa said, 'It's time I was going.'

'Oh, must you?' Shirley looked disappointed. 'I was just going to tell you about my sister's wedding.'

'Sorry, Shirley, but I must.' Lisa smiled. 'It's been a tiring day.'

Karen rose. 'I must go too. Could you phone for a taxi?' she asked Ben.

He jumped up. 'I'll take you,' he offered. 'There's only one taxi and it's bound to be taken.'

What could Lisa do, except offer to take Karen herself when she was going that way? 'You don't need to do that, Ben. I'll take her.'

'Well. . .'

'No arguments.' Lisa smiled.

'OK. Thanks.' He was pleased. His leg had been aching and he did not relish the prospect of a double drive.

Karen was effusive in her thanks for the meal.

'Come again soon,' Shirley said, standing with her arm through Ben's as they stood at the front door. 'Ian's not married.'

'They all laughed.

Lisa put the hood of the sports car up. It was always cool in the evening, even when the sun shone during the day. But as they took their seats she wished she had left it down, for it enclosed her in an intimacy with Karen that she found abhorrent.

They waved goodbye.

It was still light, but Karen's side of the car seemed to darken as they sped along the road. It was only a cloud, but Lisa shivered.

'Well, well — little Lisa.' There was no pretence in Karen's voice now. 'Fancy Daddy leaving you this island.' Her tone was sarcastic. 'And all that money as well. Tut, tut.' Her tongue clicked on her teeth.

Lisa did not answer, but concentrated on the road.

'No wonder James wants to marry you. He'd do anything for the hospital. He's a devoted doctor. I remember him saying he could do with a rich wife.'

Lisa refused to allow Karen's poisonous words to affect her. 'You'll have to do better than that,' she said in an even tone. 'James is in love with me.'

'Really?'

Lisa swerved hard to avoid a rabbit. Karen had been so intent on watching the effect of her words on Lisa's face that she had not seen the animal. She hit her head against the side-window.

Lisa was delighted. Perhaps that would stop Karen making any more insidious remarks. That 'Really?' spoken in just the right tone, had been too much.

Karen was silent until they reached the hospital. As soon as Lisa parked, she left the car without a word.

A longing to see James drew Lisa into the hospital. She would not admit that Karen's words had made her seek reassurance. She just told herself that she wanted to touch him, feel the security of his arms around her.

Lisa slipped past Reception, along the corridor and up the stairs — and then she wished she had just gone home, for it was Karen in the circle of James's arms. Karen whose face he was touching so tenderly.

Lisa turned with a stifled cry and ran down the stairs.

CHAPTER ELEVEN

LISA slept late next morning, having spent most of the night tossing in the bed. The phone ringing woke her. She reached for the receiver, thinking she was on duty and had it to her ear before she remembered she was off.

It was James. 'Lisa.' His voice sounded almost as if it was in the room.

Her heart ached with misery. She wanted to slam the receiver down, but just the sound of his voice held her.

'What on earth made you run off like that?' he asked, his angry tones bouncing off her eardrum.

'I didn't want to interrupt such a tender scene,' Lisa said sarcastically.

'Don't be silly. I was just examining the bruise your careless driving left on Karen's forehead,' he said snappily.

'My careless driving!' She was furious. 'Well!' This time she did slam the receiver down.

The phone rang again immediately, but she pulled the duvet over her head and let it ring.

How I hate Karen, she said to herself, grinding her teeth.

As soon as the ringing stopped, she threw back the duvet and climbed out of bed. She unplugged the phone, then showered, dressed in jeans and navy blue T-shirt, and went downstairs, where she unplugged the phone in the hall.

Later, in the kitchen, she was munching toast at the table when a hammering on the back door startled her.

It was the holiday season and Jean had warned her that sometimes people mistook the house for a hotel.

Lisa wished she had Rory here to protect her. There was a stout walking-stick beside the back door. She gripped it in one hand as she opened the door with the other. It might be Archie, but she wanted to be prepared.

It wasn't Archie, it was James. The anger left his face as soon as he saw the stick, and he grinned.

'Planning to bruise me now?'

Lisa raised the stick. 'Don't tempt me,' she said, her face tightening at his remark.

James took it from her and stood it against the wall. What an aggravating woman she could be. His anger returned at her cool reception.

Lisa had resumed her seat and was drinking her cooled tea, ignoring him. Controlling his anger with difficulty, he said quietly, 'Aren't you going to offer me a cup?'

'Help yourself.' Her tone was indifferent and she did not look at him, but continued to drink her tea.

'What have I done to upset you?' His tone was plaintive.

Her eyes opened wide as she looked up at him.

'Done?' Anger whitened her face. 'You accused me of damaging your precious Karen.'

James took a deep breath. 'She's not my precious Karen.' The patience in his voice aggravated Lisa. He sounded as if he was talking to a child.

'You're my precious, aren't you?' he said softly. Then the ridiculousness of it all made him laugh.

'You didn't have to take her in your arms to examine her bruise,' Lisa said, trying to hide her softening towards him by speaking brusquely.

'I didn't take her in my arms. I was just holding her face to the light to see the bruise more clearly.'

'Ha!' she said derisively, slamming her mug down on the table so that the remainder of her tea swished about.

James jerked to his feet, his chair upset by the force of his movement. 'Stop this right now.' His face was like thunder. 'Don't you want to marry me? Are you using this ridiculous argument over Karen to break our engagement?' He ran his fingers through his hair in exasperation. 'You are the most aggravating, mixed-up female I have ever met. If you're going to be jealous every time I look at another woman we might as well call it off now.'

How could Lisa tell him that it wasn't jealousy of Karen, but fear of her that had caused this argument — fear of her manipulative power? He would only think she was trying to excuse her jealousy.

Lisa hardly ever cried, but the thought of losing James brought silent tears. They ran down her face, dropped on to her T-shirt, making dark rings on the material.

He had his back to her and was staring out of the window, wondering at the incongruousness of the blue sky. The dissension in the kitchen should have turned it black.

When Lisa did not answer, he thought that she was agreeing with him — that she didn't want to marry him. That he would not accept and he swung round prepared to take his words back. The tears on her face made that unnecessary.

He was round the table and had taken her in his arms before another tear could fall. 'Darling,' he whispered, relief that she was not going to break their engagement giving depth to the endearment.

Lisa heard the deepness of his tone. She did not raise her face for his kiss, she was enjoying the comfort of his arms about her too much.

'I wish Karen had not accepted the appointment,' she murmured against his shirt. She felt him stiffen and wished she had not spoken, but now that she had she wished he would say, So do I, but he didn't.

Although James had not spoken the words she longed to hear he was thinking them, but Karen Carmichael was a member of staff now and could not be dismissed. He was in love with Lisa and did not want to distress her, but there was nothing he could do.

'How about another cup of tea?' he said.

Lisa searched his eyes for signs of anger, but saw only blandness. 'Yes,' she whispered, not quite satisfied.

'I'll make it,' he offered. As he set a mug of tea in front of her he said, 'What are your plans for today?'

'I thought I would sort out some of the things I want to take from the house,' she said, pushing the mug further on to the table. 'The sooner I move into your flat, the sooner work can begin.' And the sooner you will be removed from Karen's proximity, she thought.

'Good idea. When would you like me to move out?'

Like yesterday, Lisa would have liked to have told him, but said, 'Wednesday be all right?'

'Fine. It won't take long. I only keep clothes there.'

'I noticed,' she said drily.

James laughed. 'I could help you to move in if you like?'

'Not until it's been decorated and a few amenities installed,' she said, smiling.

James frowned. 'But won't that be an unnecessary expense? We'll need every penny for the hospital.'

'I remember him saying he could do with a rich wife.' Karen's words seemed suddenly to be emblazoned on his T-shirt. Lisa shook her head and the T-shirt became white again.

James thought she was shaking her head in disagreement and he snorted. 'How can you think it won't? What you'll spend on the flat could be put to better use.'

Their argument and the subsequent coolness she felt in him had disturbed her, but his tone made her furious and she said. 'Just because you liked to live like a Spartan doesn't mean to say that I want to.'

His face tightened. 'I lived like that because I did not want to use any of the hospital budget decorating it.' Each word was clipped.

'So. . .?' she said airily. 'I'm remedying that now.'

She was going to decorate the flat herself and just paint the kitchen. She had no intention of employing a decorator, but she wasn't going to tell James that now.

'I'd better get going,' he said, not trusting himself to speak further. 'It's my Sunday to look in on Sheena.' He smiled down at Lisa, but his smile was a little tight. 'Want to come?'

She would have loved to go with him and even rose from the table, but she did not move towards him. Instead she said, softly, sadly, 'Will my money always come between us?' She wanted him to say, Of course not. The money does not matter. All that matters is our love for each other, and for him to take her into his arms, but he was looking at her thoughtfully as he said, 'Not if we can agree on the way you spend it.'

His answer clutched at her heart, making it—not ache, but fill with pain. His words convinced her that he did not love her. He only loved what her money could do. Her suspicions had been correct.

If James had known how she would interpret his words he would not have spoken. His love for her was not connected with her money.

Lisa felt the room swirl and sat down abruptly. 'I won't go to Sheena's.' It was only her grit that enabled her to speak at all.

Her voice sounded calm—detached, and James

frowned. He sensed that his words had upset her and couldn't understand why.

'Coming to see me away?' he said, putting on a bright face.

Lisa did not want him to see that she suspected, mistakenly, the real reason for his proposal, so rose and joined him, but her legs felt like an old woman's as she moved.

James put his arm around her and she leant against him, needing his support, and as she did so the fresh smell of him filled her nostrils and she could have cried because she knew, suddenly, that she would marry him regardless—knew that she must be with him no matter what. Her fighting spirit was not strong enough to overcome losing him.

Outside, she raised her face to his. His eyes were unreadable, but his kiss when it came was fierce in its passion.

What did it matter if he did not love her? He wanted her and that would have to do.

Lisa decorated the flat and James, seeing her do it herself, was pleased. He thought he was responsible until he complimented her upon her economy.

'I meant to do it myself anyway.' She spoke with spirit.

When she moved in, work on Halliman House could be started after planning permission had been granted.

She had arranged for Jean and Archie to be given generous pensions.

'If you ever need a housekeeper,' Jean had said with a smile, 'don't hesitate to call me.'

'I won't.' Lisa had given her a hug. 'I'll miss your cooking.'

Karen wasn't at all pleased to see James move out and Lisa take his place in the room opposite.

Ian was in hospital for ten days. Lisa wanted to make quite sure his wound was healed before she discharged him.

When she visited him on Tuesday, she said, 'I think you should convalesce with your brother so that I can keep an eye on you.' She smiled. 'If you do, we'll let you go tomorrow.'

'You can keep an eye on me any time you like,' he said with a grin. 'I'll stay.' He was sitting in an armchair in the side-ward. He had lost weight, but this added to his attractiveness.

Lisa laughed. 'I was being selfish really. If you're on the island we can consult you professionally.'

'Alas. And here was I thinking that you wanted me for myself.' His sad expression was spoilt by the laughter in his eyes.

James came in at that moment. He was aware that Lisa's and Ian's sense of humour was different from his own and he tried not to let it bother him, but he felt excluded now and this made him say, looking at Lisa, 'While you are joking, one of your patients is waiting.'

Lisa turned a laughing face to his, but her smile died as she saw him. 'Well, it is my coffee time,' she said a little stiffly. Their relationship was still strained.

'That's what I like to hear — dedication.' His tone was cuttingly sarcastic.

'Whoops!' Ian grimaced.

James gave him a hard look and left without a word.

'He's jealous,' Ian said, quite unperturbed.

'Oh, I don't think so,' said Lisa a little wistfully. 'His work comes first.'

Ian looked surprised. 'Even before you?'

'I think so.' Lisa could not stop the sadness colouring her voice. 'James will do anything he has to for the patients' welfare.'

Ian rose to his feet and put an arm round her

shoulders. 'Ditch him,' he whispered. 'You'd always come first with me.'

Lisa laughed and pushed him away. 'Always the joker,' she said, moving towards the door.

She heard him laugh.

'I can't fool you, can I?' he said.

Lisa swung round with a grin.

'That's because I know you're only after my money,' she jested.

'Well, you must admit it's a tempting prospect.' His eyes were alight with mischief.

'Goodbye,' she said emphatically and stepped out into the corridor still laughing and bumped into James.

Had he been waiting for her? she wondered.

'What's the joke?' he asked stiffly.

Lisa's face straightened. 'Ian wants to marry me for my money,' she said, watching him closely.

'Perhaps he has the right idea,' James said in an offhand way. 'I can see how it would have possibilities for——'

'Possibilities?' Lisa interrupted him. She was furious. Her mother's, 'I only married you for your money,' and Karen's insidious remarks, coupled with her own feeling that that was why James was marrying her, surged up to the surface and she cried out the words she had promised herself she would never say.

'Is that why you're marrying me — for my money?'

Shocked, James could only stare at her.

'So that's what you think.' His jealousy of Ian was forgotten. His face whitened, his fists clenched, his body became rigid with the effort required to control his fury. 'There's not going to be any marriage.' He spat the words at her. 'How can there be a marriage where there is no trust?' Swinging on his heel, he left her, but with every step he felt pulled apart, his very being torn to shreds. He did not think of the new hospital. He did not think of what her money could do for the island. He thought only of how empty the years ahead would be. Fool—fool, to let his temper take over, but how could he compete with her lack of trust?

Good riddance, Lisa thought, angry herself now, and she turned the opposite way, which happened to be towards the medical ward. She pushed open the doors viciously and they swung wildly so that she just missed being hit in the back.

Karen's beaming face greeted her. She had heard every word. That was all Lisa needed. She turned about and pushed back through the doors.

I wish I'd never come to this island. I wish my father had not remembered me in his will. I wish—I wish. . .

She fled into the surgery, flung herself into the chair and cried bitter tears. I hate him—I hate him—I hate him. She drummed her fists on the desk. You couldn't even have a conversation with him without him flying into a rage. That it was her doubts about him that had started it she would not admit. She had been right to voice her suspicions. At least now she knew— Suddenly her anger left her. Knew what? That he was after her money? That he did not love her for herself?

Tears fell afresh. She knew nothing really, except that he was right—she was a mixed-up female. The only thing she did know was that he meant everything to her and that her life would be even more blighted now than it had been before, without him.

Taking a tissue from the box, she crossed to the sink and bathed her face in cold water. Then, when she felt more composed, she buzzed Moira for the next patient. It was Patrick Casey.

Her diagnosis had proved correct and he had been transferred to the mainland hospital. What was he doing here?

'Don't you want to see Dr James?' she asked as he sat down.

'He said I was your patient.'

The difference in Patrick was amazing. He had put on weight and his colour had improved.

Lisa flicked open his notes and stopped at the laboratory reports. His sputum was not active and the X-ray results had not been as serious as Lisa had suspected, but Patrick had discharged himself from the hospital.

She looked at him sternly. 'Do you want to kill yourself, Patrick?'

The bluntness of her words made his eyes fly open.

'No,' he said, startled.

'Well, discharging yourself from hospital is a good way to do it.' Her expression did not alter. 'You have no home and no means of support and I don't suppose you've given up drinking either.' She sounded exasperated. 'In fact I'm surprised you came to see me at all.'

'I couldn't stay in that place any longer.' There was no apology in his voice. 'I miss the sea and the sky too much.' He was wearing quite a respectable pair of jeans and a jacket that still had plenty of wear in it. It looked familiar. 'I came to get a prescription for my tablets, not a lecture,' he said sharply, his Irish accent pronounced.

Lisa could sympathise with him. She had grown to love the island — to love the sea and the sky as much as Patrick did.

'I think you should be re-admitted,' she said. 'You could have a bed here.' She smiled.

'No,' he said fiercely.

She sighed and pulled the prescription pad towards her. She wrote rapidly. 'Where are you staying?' she asked without looking up. She needed to write the address at the top of the prescription.

'At Jamie's.'

No wonder the jacket looked familiar; it was an old one of James's.

Her face showed her surprise. 'Well, why didn't you get your prescription from him?.' She was seething.

'He said it wouldn't be ethical.' Patrick shrugged.

Ethical? she thought. Was it ethical to let Patrick stay instead of packing him back to hospital?

'I see,' she said, giving him a smile which she hoped wasn't as stiff as her face. She would have to speak to James.

She handed the prescription to her patient. 'There won't be any need for me to tell you to take care of yourself if you're staying with the doctor,' she said wryly.

Patrick grinned. 'Thanks, Doc.'

She went with him to the door. 'Make an appointment to see me next week,' she said. 'I want to keep an eye on you.'

Patrick nodded.

She returned to the desk and buzzed Moira. 'Any more for me?'

'No. And Dr Jamie's finished as well.'

'Is he in his surgery?'

'Yes, but you'd better hurry if you want to catch him.'

Lisa's anger carried her as far as his door. She knocked.

'Come in.'

Suddenly the sound of his voice filled her with desolation. She was about to turn away when the door was jerked open and James stood there with the light behind him, a tall, dark, powerful figure, but this time she did not throw herself into his arms—this time she controlled herself.

'You wanted to see me?' His face was so tight she could see the outline of his jaw as he clenched his teeth.

'Yes,' she said in a haughty way. 'It was your duty to send Patrick back to hospital. Why didn't you?'

Stung by her attack on his integrity, James said, sarcastically, 'You're a great one for jumping to conclusions, aren't you?'

Lisa could have wept at the tone of his voice.

'Perhaps if you thought a little more deeply first you might see things more clearly,' he said in a clipped voice.

His words swept away her anguish. 'I feel I'm seeing things more clearly now than I ever did before.' Her eyes blazed. 'I'll give you my resignation.' And she turned to go.

Even though he was furious with her James could not stop wanting her, he only wished he could. He wanted to crush her to him now, silence her with his lips, make love to her here in the corridor.

His lips tightened and he caught hold of her arm and pulled her into his surgery. The suddenness of his action almost threw her off balance.

'Now you're being hysterical,' he said sharply.

James knew he should have let go of her, but her skin was like silk beneath his fingers and desire flared within him; however, the face that looked up at him was cool and arrogant and it effectively quenched his passion. He let go of her arm.

The tension between them was so great that the skin of their faces tightened. Lisa could bear it no longer. She felt she would break into little pieces if she did not leave this minute.

She took a step forward and James stood aside, his face as bleak as hers. He even held the door open for her.

Her full skirt brushed against his legs as she swung past him and she could have cried out in anguish as she thought that this touch would be the last she would have of him.

CHAPTER TWELVE

Much as Lisa would have liked to leave the island immediately, she knew that she could not desert the patients. They needed her. She would have to stay until either a locum or another doctor could be engaged.

That afternoon, she laid her resignation on James's desk, choosing a time when she knew he would be out on his visits to do so.

Later that evening, she was making herself some scrambled egg she did not want when James phoned.

'So you're going to leave me in the lurch,' he said, trying to hide the bleakness he was feeling by using a sarcastic tone.

Lisa had to grasp the receiver tightly to stop it from shaking. 'Really? Now who's jumping to conclusions?' She could not keep the bitterness out of her voice as she repeated the words he had used to her.

'I would have no hesitation about leaving you, as you say, in the lurch, but the patients are a different matter. I'll stay until you can get someone to replace me.'

'Well, unfortunately, that might not be for some time,' he said harshly. 'It's the holiday season. The locums will all be booked up.' And be banged down the receiver without saying goodbye.

Lisa caught hold of the anguish which threatened to engulf her and buried it deep inside her. She must not fall apart. She must use her vocation like a lifeline to support her.

Her face became grim as she forced herself to eat the scrambled egg and even managed a second round of toast. Two mugs of tea followed and she felt better.

There was a knock on the door and, thinking it might be the night nurse, Lisa hurried to open it as she was on call. It was Karen.

She was about to close it in her face, unable to cope with any snide remarks, when Karen's hand on the side of the door stopped her.

'An emergency has just come in,' she said.

Lisa opened the door wider.

'A woman, Amanda King, with a badly infected arm. She'll need antibiotics.'

Lisa did not doubt Karen, for, no matter how much she hated the dark-haired girl, she knew she would not lie in this instance, and went with her immediately.

'She's on holiday, staying in a holiday croft,' Karen explained.

Lisa nodded.

They entered the treatment-room. A young woman of about Lisa's age lay on the couch with an auxiliary nurse beside her.

'You can go now, Nurse,' Karen said.

As the auxiliary left the room, Karen introduced Lisa to the patient. 'This is Dr Halliman. She would like to take a look at your arm.' She glanced at Lisa. 'Miss Amanda King.'

'Hello,' said Lisa, with a smile. The patient's name sounded familiar. She took a closer look at the thin young woman whose pale complexion was brightened by the flush on her cheeks. Her hair was brown and shoulder-length. Her T-shirt and jeans were clean, but showed signs of wear. A well-washed anorak lay on the chair.

'You don't recognise me,' Amanda said, but did not smile.

Amanda King? Then Lisa remembered. Amanda had been a medical student with her, but had dropped medicine abruptly in her fifth year. Lisa had not seen her since.

She smiled. 'Now I do,' she said and bent her head to look at Amanda's arm; she knew immediately how it had become so badly infected. Amanda was a drug addict. There were needle marks on her arm.

Lisa glanced up at Karen, who was watching her, an amused expression in her eyes. She had known and had not warned her.

Lisa's eyes narrowed. 'How long has your arm been like this, Amanda?' Her face was stern, but not uncompassionate.

Amanda shrugged. 'I don't know.' She seemed uninterested.

Lisa looked at Karen. 'Anyone with her?'

'A man brought her in. He said he'd wait in the van outside.'

'He's probably gone,' Amanda said, showing some emotion this time.

A dressing trolley was standing ready, but there weren't any gloves on the bottom shelf. Lisa looked pointedly at Karen, who gave her a mocking smile and crossed over to a shelf where sterile packs of gloves were kept. Lisa knew Karen had left the gloves off on purpose.

She waited until the gloves were placed on the trolley, then said, 'I won't need these,' with an expressionless face.

'I just want to feel in her axilla.'

I really must not lower myself to her level, Lisa thought, but was pleased to see Karen blush.

Turning to the patient, she said, 'I just want to see if the glands under you arm are swollen.'

Amanda shrugged, but a grimace crossed her face as she moved her arm.

The glands were swollen. 'Have you take her temperature?' Lisa asked in a cool voice as she washed the smell of sweat from her hands.

Karen pushed the notes in front of Lisa. Amanda's temperature was thirty-nine. Lisa went back to the patient. 'I think we should admit you. You have a temperature, your arm's badly infected and you'll need antibiotics.' Her face softened. 'And someone to take care of you.'

Alarm brightened Amanda's eyes. 'Julian will look after me. Just give me a prescription and some dressings.' She swung her legs over the side of the couch. 'I'll manage.'

Lisa doubted very much that Amanda would and tried again to persuade her to be admitted, but the young woman was adamant.

'Well, I'll arrange for the nurse to visit you,' Lisa said.

But again it was useless. Amanda refused. 'No — no,' she cried, becoming hysterical.

'All right — all right,' Lisa said in a calm voice. 'We won't force you.' She encouraged Amanda to lie down again. 'Sister will give you an injection.'

Amanda's eyes widened.

'Penicillin,' Lisa told her wryly.

Amanda relaxed.

'She'll apply a dressing and give you some to take away.' Lisa looked at her patient sternly. 'I want to see you again to make sure you're getting better.'

'All right.' Amanda gave an impatient sigh.

Lisa drew Karen out of earshot. 'Put an ichthammol dressing on her arm and a sling. I don't suppose telling her to remove the sling at intervals so that her arm won't stiffen will do any good, but tell her anyway. She'll probably take the sling off as soon as she leaves.'

Karen nodded. There was no mockery in her face. She was the professional nurse now and good at her job. 'Give her an injection of triplopen. That should hold her for a day or two.' Lisa frowned. 'We'll need to see her then, though.'

Karen nodded and left Lisa to write up the notes.

She had just capped her pen when a man burst in. He was tall and wiry and about thirty years of age. His brown hair was conventionally cut and his blue eyes were the colour of his jeans. He was wearing a T-shirt and a denim shirt on top.

'I'm not waiting any longer,' he said, scowling at Amanda. 'I'm off,' and he swung about, knocking the trolley so that it skittered towards Karen who caught it.

'No, Julian.' Amanda's voice was desperate. She slid off the couch and ran after him, her arm in the sling wafting.

Lisa recognised that cry. It was from the heart, and her own anguish, which she thought she had successfully controlled, rose up to swamp her and held her immobile.

Karen had her back to the door, clearing the trolley. She swung round. 'Why didn't you stop her?'

The sharpness of her voice shook Lisa out of her agony. She rushed through Reception and out of the hospital, but she was too late. The van was just turning into the road. She would never be able to catch it.

Feeling like a soldier who had deserted his post, Lisa went back into the hospital, her head hanging, her loose hair falling forward to hide her face.

'You're not much of a doctor,' Karen said in a derisive way. 'I've reported you to James.'

This brought Lisa's head up. She threw back her hair. 'How dare you?' she said, her blue eyes fierce.

Karen was not dismayed. 'I'm the senior sister in charge of this hospital and have every right to report a doctor's incompetence.'

In this, Karen was right, but the case had not been

handled incompetently. Nothing except force would have stopped Amanda King from leaving.

There was no point in arguing with Karen, so Lisa said, 'I'll be in the flat if you need a doctor,' in a cold voice.

'Huh,' was Karen's reply.

Lisa had just made a cup of tea when the front door opened and James strode into the kitchen. I must get that second key off him, Lisa thought inconsequentially as James, his face white with anger, said, 'What's this I hear about you mistreating a patient?'

Lisa tried to steady the sudden fluttering of her heart. His anger had not alarmed her, it had excited her. There was such passion in it, and memories of their wild lovemaking threatened to throw her into his unwilling arms. She had to hold herself in check.

Before she could reply, he said, 'Why did you let a patient with a severe infection leave the hospital?'

Lisa was livid. 'The way you did Patrick?'

The severity of James's expression should have made Lisa tremble, but she was too angry and glared at him.

'Patrick Casey came over on my father's ferry. He said that he could stay a while. Father had helped Patrick before.'

Suddenly, Lisa had that outsider feeling again. The islanders looked after their own. It was nobody's business but theirs as to how or why they did it.

'Nobody could have kept Amanda,' Lisa said in a controlled voice.

'Just as no one could have prevented Patrick.' James's tone had quietened.

Lisa's face was stiff with tension. The blue of her eyes had darkened like the sun leaving a summer's sky. There was a disheartened look about her. James longed to reach out for her, but too much, yet not enough, had happened between them.

She turned away from him. A silence fell between them, but it was a silence filled with longing. It needed just a look or a gesture to throw them into each other's arms, but their pride — his Scottish, hers Halliman — held them apart.

James closed his eyes for a moment, then said, 'Don't you think we'd better go and check on her?'

Lisa looked over her shoulder at him, her face partially hidden by her hair. She expected to see disapproval in his eyes, but there was just sadness.

'I'll go,' she said, taking a step forward.

'No.' His voice was firm. 'We'll both go.'

Was he doubting her ability? Did he think he had to check up on her?

She was just about to challenge him when he said, 'We'll take Rory with us.' And she remembered him saying that Rory was a deterrent to possible attackers, especially against drug addicts tempted by a doctor's bag.

She collected her jacket and together, yet miles apart, they stood outside Karen's door. She opened it to James's knock and her eyes gleamed when she saw Lisa's tense expression. She assumed that it was due to James's displeasure, unaware that it was his nearness that was tightening Lisa's face.

'We're going to check on Miss King,' Lisa said. 'You can contact us on the car phone if you need us.'

'Very well.' Karen spoke to James, giving him a big smile. She ignored Lisa.

James nodded, but did not return her smile. Karen had been right to phone him, but he had not liked the note of satisfaction he had heard in her voice. Perhaps he had been too hasty in his assumption that Lisa's dislike of Janet's niece was because she was jealous. There seemed to be more between these two.

But all thoughts of Karen left him as Lisa took her

seat beside him. He was grateful the dog was with them. It would relieve the tension.

Rory almost jumped from the back seat, where he had been napping, in his excitement at seeing Lisa. James envied the affection he saw on her face and the eagerness with which she accepted Rory's kisses and wished he were receiving the caress she was giving to the dog.

The gear-lever grated as he pushed it clumsily into first. Damn, he thought, and concentrated more fully as he drove away from the hospital.

The high beam bathed the darkness, washing some of the blackness away, but replacing it with an unreality. It seemed almost as if they were driving in a dream; only Rory's hot breath on the back of her neck reassured Lisa that it wasn't.

Lights were on in the croft as they drew up, and voices broke the silence. An argument stopped abruptly before Lisa and James could hear what was said.

The door was flung open. A man's silhouette, legs apart, fists clenched, threw its shadow towards them. It was as if he had lunged to attack and Rory growled.

'What do you want?' The voice was hostile and the dog would have leapt if James had not had a tight hold on his collar.

'I'm Dr James McKinnon. Dr Halliman you know.' His voice was firm, his face stern. 'We're here to persuade Miss King to return with us to the hospital.' His tone softened slightly as he said, 'She's a very sick woman.'

'No. She doesn't need medical attention. She can look after herself.' Julian jerked his head in Lisa's direction. 'Ask her,' and he slammed the door.

'What did he mean?' James said as they walked towards the Range Rover. The headlights shone on Lisa's face. It was expressionless.

'Amanda King was a medical student with me, but she dropped out in her fifth year. I suppose she thinks she has enough medical knowledge to look after herself.'

'Why didn't you tell me you knew her?'

'I never thought of it. It was a long time ago.' She bent to pat Rory, but James thought she did it to avoid his eyes.

'Was that the only reason?'

Her head shot up. 'What other reason could there be?' she asked sharply.

When he did not answer, but just kept staring at her with a bleak expression on his face, she said, having difficulty controlling her voice — she wanted to scream at him, 'Surely you don't think I supply her with drugs?'

'Why did she choose Bruig for a holiday?' The awfulness of his suspicion forced the words from his mouth before he could stop them.

'Ohh!' An agonised cry was torn from her. 'How can you accuse me of lacking in trust?'

James reached out a hand, but she shrank away and rushed to the Range Rover. She was not going to sit beside him and scrambled on to the back seat with the dog. Rory licked the tears from her face and made little whining noises which she wished she could make herself — keening for the death of her loved one, for that was how she must think of James. He would be dead for her from now on.

Whey they arrived back, Karen met them in Reception.

'I've just taken a phone call for you, Lisa.' Her face was set in sympathetic lines, but her eyes were cold. 'Your mother's in hospital.' She named a famous private clinic in London. 'She's dying of cancer and would like to see you. The doctor said she's not got long to live.'

CHAPTER THIRTEEN

LISA had not seen her mother since she was at school. Zara Halliman was a stranger. It was bizarre that her dying mother should rescue her from an intolerable situation now.

'You can fly from Glasgow,' she heard James say. 'The first ferry crosses at six in the morning.'

Lisa ignored him and left him with Karen, who had transferred her sympathetic expression to him.

She undressed and fell into bed, but her night was wretched, haunted by desires and intolerable longings.

Rising at five, she dressed in the white outfit she had worn on her arrival, drank a cup of coffee and was in her car by five-thirty.

Duncan met her at the ferry. Lisa had not seen him since their first meeting. She had wondered about this, for she had expected James to invite her to dinner at his house when his father had been there.

Duncan greeted her with highland courtesy but not with the familiarity she would have expected if James had told him about the engagement. Had James meant to break it off? Still, what did that matter now?

Lisa left the car at Glasgow airport, and on her arrival in London took a taxi to the clinic. She was taken immediately to her mother's bedside.

The journey down had been spent in a vacuum, as far as Lisa was concerned, but the sight of her mother's frailness shook her out of it. The heartache started, not only for the loss of James, but for the coming death of her mother.

Lisa forgot the empty years, the lack of love, in compassion for the dying woman.

The beauty which had made her mother a famous model was still there in the fine bone-structure, but the skin was yellowed and the closed eyes were sunken. Zara Halliman was fifty-three, but she looked ten years older. Her hair had been skilfully dyed to almost its original light brown colour. She was wearing a pale pink frothy nightgown and her nails were painted the same colour. It was an act of bravery to appear normal.

Lisa had already been told by the doctor that her mother was having injections of morphia to control the pain, and that she might be too heavily sedated to recognise her.

The nurse said, 'Your daughter is here, Mrs Halliman.'

The seriously ill woman opened her eyes and looked at Lisa. 'Lisa,' she whispered and smiled.

Lisa sat in a chair placed for her and did not even hear the door close behind the nurse.

'Can you forgive me?' The whispered words fell like dying leaves.

Lisa took the thin, cold hand in her warm ones.

'Yes.' Her voice sounded loud in the thick-carpeted, double-glazed room.

Zara sighed and closed her eyes. For a moment, Lisa thought her mother had died and gripped the hand in hers.

Zara opened her eyes again. 'I loved your father, you know,' she said simply. 'Those other men meant nothing to me.'

Consternation engulfed Lisa. All these years she had supposed — 'But you said you only married him for his money,' she cried, unable to contain her shock.

'It was a lie.' Zara's eyes filled with sadness. 'I wanted to hit back at him. I knew he had mistresses, and then, after the divorce, I sought solace elsewhere, but it was no good.'

'Oh, Mother.' Lisa laid her head down beside Zara. Tears slipped down her cheeks on to the pillow. Tears for her mother's painful years without Charles and tears for the painful years to come for herself, without James. She wished she could die with her mother. At least they would both be at peace then.

Zara's hand tightened in Lisa's, not in pain, but in love. Lisa sat up, fresh tears for what might have been between them falling on to her white dress like raindrops.

She reached for a tissue from the box on top of the locker and wiped her face. When she realised that she was crying for herself, the tears stopped. This would help neither her mother nor herself. Zara needed her daughter's strength.

So Lisa watched over her mother and when the hand in hers tightened in pain this time she rang the bell. The nurse came with an injection, but Zara would not let her give it. She wanted to say something else. Lisa bent closer.

'I want you to know how proud I am of you. I wanted to say this to you when you qualified, but I felt that too many years had passed.'

Lisa kissed her mother. She saw the lines of pain deepen and gestured for the nurse to give the injection.

The next few hours were harrowing. Her mother's pain was kept under control with the drugs so that she did not suffer. It was Lisa who did the suffering.

As time went by her mother became confused and thought it was Charles who was sitting beside her, Lisa's looks were so akin to his.

The next day, exactly twenty-four hours after Lisa's arrival, her mother died peacefully with her hand in her daughter's.

The sister handed Lisa an envelope and a bunch of keys after formalities had been observed. 'The keys are to Mrs Halliman's London flat,' she said, looking kindly upon the exhausted young woman. 'This letter is for you.'

Lisa left, glad to leave behind this private clinic with its façade of luxury behind which death lurked.

She opened the letter in Harrods' café. A further letter inside was for the lawyer. Her mother's writing threatened to bring more tears. The letter contained all that her mother had told her daughter. It had been written in case Lisa had not come.

She was exhausted. A few catnaps had carried her through while she sat with her mother.

A taxi took her to the Knightsbridge flat. It was luxurious, but modern. The décor was white and honey. Simple but expensive furniture in light ash added to the airiness of the atmosphere.

Her mother seemed to be everywhere. Photographs taken when Zara was a model—more recent ones posing with young men were arranged to their best advantage.

In her mother's bedroom a portrait of Lisa's father hung over the bed. She would have liked to cut it to pieces, but she knew such an action would have distressed her mother.

She turned her back on the face so like her own and opened mirrored doors that ran the length of one wall. Clothes for every occasion with matching shoes, bags and hats filled the whole wall-space.

Lisa pressed her face into the soft folds of a white silk dress. Her mother's perfume filled her nostrils. She remembered it from childhood.

She threw herself down on the bed, and a fierce longing for James gripped her. The white silk bedspread reminded her of the white rug they had made love on and, unable to bear the anguish any longer, she sprang from the bed and left the room.

In the large, fully automated kitchen Lisa searched for coffee. She found it and made herself a drink, thankful that the water and electricity had not been turned off.

In the lounge she found a Chinese lacquered drinks cabinet and poured herself a large whisky. She took it with her and left it beside the bed in the spare room.

She showered in the blue tiled bathroom, dried herself on a thick blue towel and drew a towelling dressing-gown of the same colour about her.

The spare room was decorated in pink. Lisa slid back the mirrored doors, the same as in her mother's room, and found a selection of clothes all in her size. Had her mother prepared this room for her? Lisa wondered.

Grief caught her afresh and she threw off the robe, slipped on a silk nightdress she found in the well-filled drawers and climbed into bed.

She took the glass. Tears dropped into the amber liquid as she gazed into its depths, but there was nothing to see, nothing to help her. She drank the whisky, turned out the light and closed her eyes.

Emotional exhaustion coupled with the whisky ensured that she slept well.

The next few days were spent seeing to her mother's affairs and visiting the lawyer. A few people she did not know attended the funeral, but the one person Lisa longed for was not there — James.

The July heat in London was oppressive. Lisa felt suffocated and longed for the island, for the fresh breezes, the dramatic scenery. It wasn't just because James was there. Bruig called to her.

On Thursday Lisa locked up the flat. She would need it if she decided to return here to work.

She was hot and sticky by the time she reached the

airport; even her silver-grey sleeveless dress felt damp. She had struggled out of a matching jacket in the taxi and nearly tripped over it as it fell from her arm. It was an outfit she had found among the clothes in the pink room. Her mother must have known her sizes and the poignancy of the care with which the clothes had been chosen had brought fresh tears to Lisa's eyes as she had dressed that morning.

If only she had known. Then she was shocked at the arrogance of her thought. If she had contacted her mother she would have known.

The weather was still hot when she reached Glasgow. Lisa knew she should have rung James from London to let him know when she was to arrive at the hospital, but she was too disheartened. The Scottish accents of the people soothed her to some extent.

The drive north passed quickly. This time she caught the main ferry and arrived at the hospital at four o'clock. She climbed stiffly out of the car. James and the locum would be about to start the evening surgery.

She decided not to disturb James. She would see him later. She knew she was putting off the moment, but felt she would be able to face him better after a shower.

Moira was on Reception when Lisa entered the hospital. 'Am I glad you're back,' she said with a sigh. 'It's been murder since you left. Dr James couldn't get a locum. They were all booked up.' Then she gave Lisa a sympathetic smile. 'I'm sorry about your mother. We all saw the notice in the *Scotsman*.'

'Thanks, Moira,' Lisa said. The lack of a locum meant that she would have to relieve James now. He must be exhausted. 'Is James in?'

'Five minutes ago.'

There were already four patients waiting. Lisa smiled at them as she passed through the reception area.

Outside James's door, she took a deep breath and knocked.

'Come in.'

The sound of his voice with its Scottish lilt brought back all the old longings. Lisa wanted and yet did not want to enter the surgery. Her mouth became dry. She would be unable to speak and panic gripped her, but she would have to go in now. She turned the handle and entered.

James was seated at the desk with Karen standing beside him. The faces they turned to Lisa were smiling, but she felt sure that the smile was not for her, but for each other. It vanished when they saw her.

It appeared as if Karen had made good use of Lisa's absence. It was no good telling herself that she did not care. Lisa did.

'You might have let us know you were coming back,' Karen said. It sounded as if she had not expected Lisa to return at all.

'Why? Did you think I wouldn't?'

The bluntness of her reply jolted Karen.

James had risen when she entered. His face had thinned and had lost its tan. He looked tired. There was a bleakness about his eyes that Lisa knew as if he had told her himself was due to suppressed longing. He still wanted her.

Lisa had thought that her love for James had died, but it was there as strong as ever, filling her whole being, lighting her soul, lifting her spirits. No matter how hard she tried to suppress it, it would not be denied and she only hoped that it did not show in her eyes.

'I was sorry to hear of your mother's death,' James said. The effort required to subdue his flaring desire made his voice sound trite.

It was this triteness that helped Lisa to control herself. 'Thank you,' she said, her face expressionless.

Her blonde hair sat in waves about her shoulders. Her grey outfit was softly feminine. She had applied more make-up than usual to give her confidence, but it was muted. Her lipgloss was a delicate shade of pink. She had lost weight, and to James she appeared fragile. If Karen had not been there. . .

'Moira told me that you didn't manage to get a locum,' said Lisa. 'I'll take over now and be on call tonight.'

James wanted to protest. Lisa had had a long journey and must be tired herself, but her withdrawn expression and the firmness with which she had spoken prevented him.

'Good,' said Karen brightly. 'You can give me the dinner you promised now, James.' She did not like the way he was looking at Lisa. It wasn't the expression in his eyes that bothered her; they were bland enough. It was the way his body leaned ever so slightly towards Lisa. It was as if his body was trying to say what unspoken words could not.

James pulled himself upright. 'Yes,' he said. 'Good idea. Thanks, Lisa. We'll be at the Bruig Arms if you need anything.' He gestured to the case-notes on the desk. 'You might as well use this surgery.'

Lisa nodded and stood aside for them to pass. She put her shoulder-bag down on the desk and as the door closed sat down in James's vacated seat. It was still warm.

His presence was all around her. His stethoscope was on the desk, his pen beside the prescription pad. His doctor's white coat, which he put on if he wanted to inspect a wound, lay over the end of the couch. His doctor's bag was on the chair.

She could collect the notes and go to her own surgery, but she was held in this room by his presence.

There was a knock on the door followed by Moira popping her head round. 'Ready to start?'

'Yes.' Lisa smiled. 'Send in the first one.'

It was Kirsty McLean with her son Kevin for his periodic check-up. 'That's fine,' said Lisa, checking the little boy's finger movement.

'Thank you, Doctor,' Kirsty grinned. Then her face straightened. 'Sorry about your mother.'

'Thanks, Kirsty.'

Lisa supposed everyone on the island knew and felt comforted, accepted, and knew she did not want to leave Bruig.

It was quite a busy surgery. There was an antitetanus injection to be given to a patient who had cut her finger opening a corned beef tin. Two summer visitors who had stayed too long in the sun and had blistered shoulders which needed dressing. A case of suspected glandular fever, and a few more patients with minor complaints.

It was six o'clock when she saw the last patient out. The notes written up, she took them along to Moira.

'I don't suppose you've any milk?' she asked hopefully. 'I collected some food on the way up, but forgot the milk.'

Moira reached behind a pile of case-notes and handed Lisa a pint of milk. 'I hope its OK and not sour,' she said with a smile.

Lisa gave her a grateful smile as she took it. 'You know I'm on call tonight?'

'Yes, James told me.'

It required two journeys to collect her things from the car. She was passing Reception the second time when she paused and said, 'By the way, what happened to Amanda King?'

Moira thought for a moment. 'As far as I know she left the island. Do you want her notes?'

'No, thanks,' said Lisa hastily.

Lisa unpacked, made herself a salad and a cup of tea, showered and lounged in her dressing-gown to watch television. The programme did not hold her so she turned off the set and went to bed.

George McCallan was on switchboard duty during the night. The phone beside Lisa's bed rang. She switched on the light and reached for the receiver.

'There's an Amanda King on the phone, Doctor,' George said. 'She sounds pretty desperate. Says the infection in her arm has flared up again.'

'What time is it, George?' Lisa had forgotten to wind her clock.

'One o'clock,' he said.

'Ohh,' Lisa groaned.

'Do you want me to pass it on to Dr Jamie?' George asked. Then his tone softened. 'I heard about your mother. I'm very sorry.'

'Thanks, George, but I think Dr Jamie has done enough. I'll go.'

Lisa dressed in jeans, a fine woollen jumper and blue anorak, picked up her doctor's bag and went down to George.

'Here you are, Doctor,' he said, handing her the notes. 'I'll have a cup of tea ready for you when you get back.'

'Thanks.'

Lisa was at the door when George called after her, 'Don't you think you'd better take Rory?'

Lisa swung round. 'Is he here?'

'Dr Jamie said he would collect him when he leaves.'

When he leaves? thought Lisa. He must be with Karen. Oh, how her heart ached.

CHAPTER FOURTEEN

'WELL , if he's there,' she managed to say in a normal voice.

George left the counter and Lisa could hear him saying, 'Come on, old boy. Wake up.'

'Leave him, George,' she called.

But the next minute Rory had bounded over the reception counter, scattering papers as he did so, in his eagerness to reach Lisa. Paws were up at her shoulders in a minute and he was licking her as if he had never seen her before.

Lisa laughed. 'Down, Rory,' she commanded. Immediately he dropped to the floor, his tail wagging, a big grin on his face.

George handed her the lead and she clipped it on. Once in the Range Rover, he settled down.

It was a clear night following a clear day, but not bright enough for her to use only the low beam. She knew how tricky the bends in the road were.

The croft was on the other side of the island and she was glad she had gone with James before, as it was tucked round a bend up a bumpy track.

As soon as she arrived she sensed something was wrong. The croft was the same and there was a light on, but there was just something odd about it, and she was glad she had Rory with her.

Taking the lead firmly in her hand, she collected her doctor's bag and left the Range Rover, regretting that she had not thought to remove the syringe and needles from the equipment in the boot. They would be a temptation to a drug addict.

Then she chided herself for her suspicions. It was almost as bad as James accusing her of being a supplier. However, she decided to leave Rory on guard at the rear of the Range Rover and said, in a commanding voice. 'Sit — guard.'

She expected the front door to be open when she reached it. Amanda must have heard her arrive. Stilling her beating heart, Lisa knocked on the door.

It was too stout for her to hear footsteps, so she was taken by surprise when it jerked open and Julian grabbed her arm, pulling her inside.

'Hey!' she cried, trying to pull away, but his grasp was too tight.

'Give me the bag,' he said in a menacing tone.

She swung it at him, meaning to hit him with it, but it was too heavy and moved in slow motion so that he was able to grasp it.

Lisa would not let it go, so he jerked her forward and she would have lost her balance if he had not been holding her with his other hand. Her grip on the bag loosened.

'Let her go,' cried Amanda, rushing into the hall.

'Shut up.' Julian's voice was rough. 'Get into the lounge,' he commanded and, pulling Lisa with him, flung her into one of the armchairs. She rubbed her arm, sure that his fingers must have left a bruise.

'You won't find what you're looking for in there,' Lisa said in as firm a voice as she could muster, watching as he tipped the bag's contents on to the table. She had locked her dangerous drugs up before she had left the island and had not replaced them.

When Julian did not find what he wanted, he swept the contents off the table. They fanned about the room. He kept the syringes.

'Julian.' Amanda's tentative voice came from behind him.

He swung around. 'You idiot,' he shouted.

Amanda shrank back, wrapping her arms about her as if in protection. He strode up to her.

'It was your idea to send for this woman when you heard she was back on the island. You said she'd be easier to handle than the man.' His face was ugly in its rage.

'The car,' Amanda said, trembling, and pointed a finger towards the door. 'That's where they'll be.'

He swung about. 'Make sure she doesn't move,' he said over his shoulder as he went through the door.

Lisa looked at Amanda who was sitting hunched up in the other chair, her knuckles against her mouth, her body trembling.

'How could you?' she said, in disgust, but even as she spoke she knew her words were wasted. Amanda's whole being was concentrated on Julian finding the drug.

Aggressive growling from Rory drew Lisa's attention away from Amanda. She jumped up and made for the door, but Amanda caught hold of her arm and pulled her back. Lisa was struggling to free herself when a heart-breaking yelp was followed by silence.

Lisa was stricken. If anything had happened to Rory. . . Extra strength broke her free from Amanda and she rushed into the hall.

The doorway was blocked by Julian with Rory hanging limply in his arms. The ceiling light was of low wattage, but it was bright enough for Lisa to see the harshness of Julian's expression. He was not looking at Lisa, but at Amanda behind her.

She pushed past Lisa. 'Well, have you got it?' She was frantic.

'No.' His voice was grim. 'But we will.' He pushed Amanda aside with his elbow and brought the dog right up to Lisa. 'I'll kill the dog if you don't go back and get what we want.' There was no mistaking the ruthlessness in his voice.

Lisa could see that Rory was still breathing and knew she must do something to stop Julian from killing the dog.

'Very well,' she said in a voice as arrogant as she could make it. 'But I must attend to the dog first.'

'You're in no position to make demands,' he said harshly.

'Do you want the drugs?' Lisa said evenly.

'Oh — do as she says,' Amanda wailed.

'Yes, why don't you?' James's dry voice came from the doorway.

The reasonableness of his tone and the suddenness of his appearance froze the group so that they looked like a photograph that the flash had caught unawares.

Then Julian swung round, blood from Rory's head wound splashing the wall. Desperation gave the man strength. He threw the dog at James, who catching Rory in his arms, staggered backwards.

Before Julian could take advantage of this, Ben Anderson had stepped forward and gripped him in an armlock.

Amanda sank to the floor, wrapped her arms about her knees and groaned.

Lisa started to tremble.

'Are you all right?' James had righted himself and was looking at her over Rory's head.

'Of course,' she snapped, unwilling for him to know how frightened she had been.

James smiled, and it was that special smile that brought the tears she had so carefully suppressed. Lisa bent down to pull Amanda to her feet so that he would not see them.

'How's Rory?' she said, turning her now composed

face to him as she stood up, her arm about the shivering woman.

'I hope he's just concussed,' James said gently. 'He'll need a few stitches, though, and an X-ray.' His face showed concern as he looked down at the dog. 'Will you take him back in the Range Rover while Ben and I take these two to the police?'

'Of course.' There was no sharpness in her voice this time.

She found a blanket in the bedroom and wrapped it round Amanda's shoulders and, taking her outside, helped the trembling girl into the passenger seat of Ben's car. He was already in the back with a sullen Julian.

James joined them. He handed Ben a piece of twine.

'Better tie his wrists,' James suggested.

'Good idea,' said Ben. Julian started to struggle with him, but Ben was a powerful man and quickly had his wrists tied.

James turned to Lisa. He took hold of her arms and pulled her towards him so that their bodies touched; the light from the car's headlights was not strong enough to see the expression in his eyes, but his whispered, 'Drive carefully, my Lisa,' in a voice soft with emotion caught at her heart, but remembering George saying, 'Dr Jamie said he would collect him when he leaves,' prevented her stiff body from responding.

James, seeing her withdrawn expression, thought she was remembering his insinuation that she was supplying drugs to Amanda. There was no time to reassure her now. Rory needed attention and he had to take Amanda and her boyfriend to the police.

'I'll see you soon,' he promised with a smile, and let her go.

Rory's still form in the back of the Range Rover

worried Lisa. She decided not to take him to the vet, who was on the other side of the town, but to take him straight to the hospital.

Once there, she asked George to carry the still unconscious animal to the X-ray room where, after X-raying the dog and examining the results, she breathed more easily when she saw that Rory did not have a fractured skull. She called on George again to carry the unconscious dog to her flat, giving him the key to let himself in, while she collected stitching equipment from the treatment-room.

George was sitting on the couch with Rory beside him when Lisa entered the flat.

'Thanks, George,' she said as she opened a folded table. 'Would you lift him on here for me, please?'

'Certainly.'

He was just leaving when Karen, wearing a pink satin dressing-gown, brushed passed him through the door.

'Did you have to make such a noise, George?' she said sharply. 'You woke me up.' She was not looking at George, her eyes were searching the flat.

Looking for James, no doubt, thought Lisa, lifting her eyes from cutting the hair around Rory's head wound.

'Sorry, Sister.' George's tone just missed being insolent, but he was gone before Karen could reprimand him.

When Karen saw what Lisa was doing she said, 'Surely that dog should be at the vet's.'

'Too far,' Lisa said shortly.

'Rubbish.' Karen's tone was dismissive. 'You're just hoping to get James back by looking after his dog.'

Lisa did not reply for, if she had, Karen would have heard the pain in her voice.

She washed her hands and opened the dressing pack, then laid out the stitching instruments. When she was ready she prayed that Rory would not regain consciousness until she had finished stitching his wound.

As she inserted each stitch she was remembering another head she had sewn up—James's. Was it only three months ago?

After the last stitch was in place and the area washed clean, Lisa sprayed the wound with a plastic sealer and turned to wash her hands. She was amazed to see Karen was still there.

'I'm surprised you haven't asked what happened,' she said coldly.

'Oh, I just assumed that you had been to supply Amanda and that Julian didn't like the dog.'

Lisa would have ignored her, but suddenly her suspicions were aroused.

'How did you know Amanda was back?'

'Oh. . .' Karen's face tightened. 'I. . .'

'You bumped into her in the town when you were shopping.' James's voice came from the door; his expression was grim. 'And you said, I quote, "Lisa's back. Perhaps she can help you." But it wasn't the words, it was the way that you said them—implying that Lisa would give Amanda diamorphine.'

Karen's face became pinched with shock.

'You can't accuse me——' she started to say, but James interrupted her.

'That's exactly what I shall do if you don't pack your bags and go on the first ferry. If it weren't for your aunt's angina and the respect I have for her, I'd report you to the Royal College of Nursing.'

Karen gasped and her body stiffened. With a last look of hate directed at Lisa, she turned and left them.

'Doing another stitching job for the McKinnon family?' James said, the severe lines on his face lifting.

'Yes,' Lisa said, her voice as soft as the expression in her eyes. James took a step towards her, but before he could touch her Rory whimpered and tried to rise. They both put a hand out to stroke the dog, Lisa's reaching Rory first. James's hand fell on top of hers, and they laughed, happy laughter free suddenly from stress.

He would have taken her in his arms then, but she said, 'I think we should settle Rory.' They looked down at the dog. 'See how he trusts us?' Rory lifted a paw and Lisa took it.

'Yes', said James, his face serious. 'Animals are far more trusting than humans.'

She looked at him and smiled cheekily, 'And far less hassle. They give you their love, unreservedly.'

He grinned. 'If I promise to, from now on, will you help me to take Rory home?'

Lisa's face gave him his answer. Her expression was full of joy.

They wrapped Rory in the blanket and put him in the back of the Range Rover and Lisa sat with him. James ran back to tell George where they were going. He returned and climbed into the driver's seat.

'Just as a matter of interest,' said Lisa as he drove expertly across the island, 'what took you so long?'

'So long?' There was puzzlement in James's voice.

'Yes,' she said, 'to come from the police station.'

'Oh, that.' The Range Rover slowed to take a bend. 'I left my car at Ben's so I had to go back and collect it.

'Oh.' That explained James's delay, but not why he was at the hospital at one o'clock in the morning. She decided to wait until they had reached his home before asking him.

'My father's on holiday visiting his sister in Edinburgh,' he said as they drew up in front of the house.

The silence as the engine was turned off was broken only by the sound of the sea. It was three-thirty in the morning and the air was fresh and clean. Lisa took a deep breath. The excitement of hearing James promising to love her unreservedly had swept away her tiredness.

'And Patrick?' she asked.

James glanced at her and saw a worried look in her eye. 'He's gone back into hospital — on the mainland.' He grinned. 'He took his doctor's advice.'

Lisa grinned. 'Which doctor?'

'Not the witch doctor,' he laughed. 'Your advice.'

Their laughter disturbed the dog, who looked up at them. James stroked Rory's head and said, 'Everything's all right. You're home now.' And he lifted the dog.

Lisa opened the front door and switched on the light. James took Rory straight to the kitchen and laid the dog gently in his bed, covering him with the small blanket Rory usually lay on. Then he turned to her.

'Would you like a drink.'

She walked up to him, her eyes not leaving his face. He stood quite still until she put her arms around his neck. 'No,' she whispered.

'Are you sure?' he teased, holding her close.

'Stop messing about, James, and kiss me,' she demanded.

'Oooh, I love a forceful woman,' he joked, grinning.

She was close to him, but he pulled her closer, and when his lips met hers their kiss was just a taste of the passion that would consume them. Nothing less than total communion could wipe away the anguish they had inflicted upon each other.

It did not matter that it was his house nor that he had a single bed. Their bodies became so entwined that they did not notice its narrowness.

It was as if they could not bear to lose touch, hand against hand, body against body. Then the urgency of their lovemaking culminated in a fulfilment that was made even sweeter because of what they might have lost — each other.

Throughout the night their searching insistent hands satisfied their craving for each other, so that by the time daylight shone through a gap in the curtains they were bound forever more closely than a wedding-ring whose circle had no end. No matter what the future would hold they knew that they would live in each other's hearts, and feel each other's pain.

James raised himself up on his elbow and gazed into her face. Her hair lay in wavy tresses across the pillow like sand when the tide had gone out. Her blue eyes were clear. He felt he could see into her soul, and when she smiled a languid smile he knew she belonged to him.

'Do you still think I want your money?' His eyes were laughing.

Lisa grinned mischievously. 'No. It's my body you're after.'

'You're absolutely right there,' and he bent to kiss her, and as his kiss deepened words became unnecessary.

His alarm broke them apart.

'Now I know why people go on honeymoon — no alarm clocks,' Lisa said with a laugh.

'I'll throw the clock away,' he said with a grin, reaching out for it, but she was there before him and had turned the insistent ring off.

'You do know that we're married now?' he said, smiling down at her.

Lisa saw the vulnerability in his eyes. 'Yes,' she whispered. 'This house only accepts married couples.'

He grinned in relief. 'So you will marry me?'

'We-ell.' She pretended to think.

'Stop messing about, Lisa Halliman,' he repeated the words she had used to him.

'But will you want to marry a Halliman?' she said with a smile.

'If you marry me your name won't be Halliman, it'll be McKinnon.' He grinned.

Lisa smiled, then her expression became serious.

'I was so mixed up. You see, my mother told my father that she had married him for his money,' she said. 'That's what made me think that that was your reason for wanting to marry me so soon after we had met.' She looked at him apologetically. 'But when she was dying. . .' Tears welled in Lisa's eyes, but James did not kiss them away. She needed the relief from grief that they could give her. 'I discovered that she had always loved my father and that she had only told him that to hit back at him.' She paused for a moment, then said, 'I was also afraid to marry you in case it ended in acrimony and divorce as their marriage had.' She started to shiver.

Her expression was so vulnerable that James gathered her to him, pulling the duvet over them until her shivering had stopped.

'I can't promise that everything will go smoothly for us, darling,' he whispered. 'But I believe in our love,' and he kissed her.

Some time later he said, 'Well, I suppose we'd better get up or it'll be one o'clock before we reach the hospital and although, it being Sunday, we don't have a surgery, there are patients to see.'

Mentioning the time reminded Lisa of that other one o'clock in the small hours. 'Hey,' she said, hauling herself up on to her elbow, her hair falling about her face, 'just what were you doing at the hospital this morning?' adding, because she must know, 'Were you with Karen?'

'No.' He grinned. 'I knew I wouldn't be able to sleep, so I was doing some studying and the time just went.'

'And Karen?' Lisa gave him a murderous look.

'Hey!' He put up his hand in mock-defence. 'Karen meant nothing to me. We went out a few times, but she was always running you down.' He frowned. 'What was it between you two?'

Lisa told him the truth about the swab count.

'I'm sorry I doubted you, and I'm sorry I implied you were giving Amanda drugs. I knew you couldn't do such a thing, but I was hurt by your attitude towards me. I. . .'

Lisa drew his face down to hers and kissed him.

'Shh,' she whispered.

As she drew her lips from his, he said, with a grin, 'You've forgiven me?'

'Well. . .' She pretended to think. 'You'll have to pay me.'

James laughed. 'How much, madam?'

Lisa thought for a moment. 'Six hundred kisses.'

He pulled her to him, but she pushed him away. 'In instalments.' She grinned. 'One a month for the next fifty years.'

James laughed. 'Done.' Then his face sobered. 'I'll give you the first one now,' he said softly, his eyes full of love.

It was a long kiss and when they broke apart Lisa said laughingly, 'The kiss isn't supposed to last a month.'

'Oh,' James pretended disappointment. Then he said, 'You know, I was jealous of Ian.'

'I do know.' She grinned.

'Cheeky,' he said.

'By the way, why did you say he had the right idea to be after my money?' The words had nagged her since James had spoken them.

He laughed. 'It wasn't my idea. It was his, if you remember.'

'Oh.' Satisfied, she snuggled closer.

After a pause, she said, 'What made you come to the croft?'

'I had this terrible feeling that you were in danger,' he said. 'I rushed out to George and he told me you'd gone to see Amanda.'

The simplicity with which he spoke drew tears to her eyes. 'I love you, Dr Jamie,' she said with a catch in her voice.

'I'm glad to hear that, Dr Lisa.' He grinned and kissed her.

'Even more than Bruig?' she teased.

His face was serious as he said, 'More than its heather, more than its hills, more than anything in this life.'

'Jamie,' she whispered, her eyes full of love.

His kiss when it came was as gentle as a summer's breeze, his arms about her as strong as his island's heritage.

Her heartache had gone forever.

They were married by special licence and returned to the house overlooking the sea.

The months passed and the hospital became a reality; one day James said to Lisa, as they stood arms about each other looking at the sea from their garden, 'What do you think about calling the hospital after your mother—the Zara Halliman Memorial Hospital?'

Lisa looked up into his dear face with tears in her eyes. 'What a lovely idea. Thank you, James.' She smiled. 'You give me so much.'

'Not as much as you give me,' he said with a grin. Lisa knew he was referring to her mother's estate. She had settled it on him. They had decided to keep on the London flat, though; Lisa could not bear to part with it.

'There are some things that only a man can give a woman,' she said, smiling mysteriously.

'Hmm. I know.' James grinned.

'Do you?' Lisa raised an eyebrow. 'Well, you are a doctor.'

He looked puzzled.

'I'm pregnant,' she whispered, her face alive with happiness.

'Darling.' His tone was overjoyed. 'I'm so pleased.' He kissed her gently.

When, after a time, he released her, she said, 'If it's a boy, I think we should call it Charles.' She was teasing.

'Oh, no.' He grinned. 'Our first quarrel?'

She melted in his arms. 'Never, my darling.'

They stood a little longer looking at the sea. He caught her hand and kissed its palm.

'Our love will never fade, as this scar. . .' he touched his forehead '. . .will fade. It will be here forever.'

With her head on his shoulder and their arms about each other, they turned and went into their home.

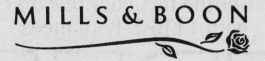

MILLS & BOON

LOVE ON CALL

The books for enjoyment this month are:

SECOND THOUGHTS Caroline Anderson
CHRISTMAS IS FOREVER Margaret O'Neill
CURE FOR HEARTACHE Patricia Robertson
CELEBRITY VET Carol Wood

❤   ❤   ❤   ❤   ❤

Treats in store!

Watch next month for the following absorbing stories:

SURGEON'S DILEMMA Margaret Barker
A LOVING LEGACY Marion Lennox
FALSE IMPRESSIONS Laura MacDonald
NEVER PAST LOVING Margaret O'Neill

Discover the thrill of *Love on Call* with 4 FREE Romances

FREE
BOOKS FOR YOU

In the exciting world of modern medicine, the emotions of true love acquire an added poignancy. Now you can experience these gripping stories of passion and pain, heartbreak and happiness - with Mills & Boon absolutely FREE! AND look forward to a regular supply of *Love on Call* delivered direct to your door.

🌷 🌷 🌷

Turn the page for details of how to claim 4 FREE books AND 2 FREE gifts!

An irresistible offer from Mills & Boon

Here's a very special offer from Mills & Boon for you to become a regular reader of *Love on Call*. And we'd like to welcome you with 4 books, a cuddly teddy bear and a special mystery gift - absolutely FREE and without obligation!

Then, every month look forward to receiving 4 brand new *Love on Call* romances delivered direct to your door for only £1.80 each. Postage and packing is FREE!

Plus a FREE Newsletter featuring authors, competitions, special offers and lots more...

This invitation comes with no strings attached. You may cancel or suspend your subscription at any time and still keep your FREE books and gifts.

It's so easy. Send no money now but simply complete the coupon below and return it today to:

Mills & Boon Reader Service, FREEPOST, PO Box 236, Croydon, Surrey CR9 9EL.

- - - - - - **NO STAMP NEEDED** - - - - - ✂ - -

YES! Please rush me 4 FREE *Love on Call* books and 2 FREE gifts! Please also reserve me a Reader Service subscription. If I decide to subscribe, I can look forward to receiving 4 brand new *Love on Call* books for only £7.20 every month - postage and packing FREE. If I choose not to subscribe, I shall write to you within 10 days and still keep the FREE books and gifts. I may cancel or suspend my subscription at any time simply be writing to you.
I am over 18 years of age.   Please write in BLOCK CAPITALS

Ms/Mrs/Miss/Mr _____ EP62D

Address _____

_____

_____ Postcode _____

Signature _____

Offer closes 31st March 1994. The right is reserved to refuse an application and change the terms of this offer. One application per household. Offer not valid to current Love on Call subscribers. Offer valid only in UK and Eire. Overseas readers please write for details. Southern Africa write to IBS, Private Bag, X3010, Randburg, 2125, South Africa. You may be mailed with offers from other reputable companies as a result of this application. Please tick box if you would prefer not to receive such offers. ☐

mps
MAILING
PREFERENCE
SERVICE